Coach Yonto nodded. "Well," he said slowly, "I'll tell you one thing right now. If you let up so much as a hair, I'll throw your butt off the team so fast you won't know what hit you."

Rudy looked at him, stunned, his mouth open. "Off the team? Did you say off the team? That means first I have to be *on* the team, right?"

"Don't let me down," said the coach.

Rudy continued to stare at Coach Yonto. "I'm on the team, right? Am I actually on the team?"

Yonto studied Rudy and wondered if he was making a mistake with this kid. He was too short to be a football player; he wasn't very fast; he wasn't very skillful—but he wanted it so badly. That was the quality that intrigued Yonto. He had never worked with a player who wanted something as badly as this kid did.

"Yeah, Ruettiger," he said. "That's what I've been saying. You're on the team."

RUDY

A TRUE STORY

A novel by
James Ellison

Based on the screenplay written by
Angelo Pizzo

BANTAM BOOKS

NEW YORK · TORONTO · LONDON · SYDNEY · AUCKLAND

RUDY

A Bantam Book / November 1993

ISBN 0-553-56528-1

Published simultaneously in the United States and Canada

PRINTED IN THE UNITED STATES OF AMERICA

OPM   0   9   8   7   6   5   4   3   2   1

*Again for Debbra, Owen, and Brett, my family.
And for David Rabinowitz, a true friend.*

ACKNOWLEDGMENTS

Special thanks to the hero of this book, Rudy Ruettiger, for his help and guidance, and to Ellen Lanser, who gave generously of her time. I would also like to thank the many officials at Notre Dame for their gracious assistance in making this novel a more accurate rendering of the university and its football program.

PART

ONE

★

1963

1

Joliet, Illinois, deep in the heart of steel-mill country, the fall of 1963 on a Saturday afternoon. Outside, the smoke-smudged sky lay low on the land, the color of slate. Soot hung over everything like a pall—cars, buildings, lawns, and fields—and shrouded what trees there were. On this particular afternoon the town was quiet, ghostlike, the streets gray and lifeless, just the occasional soul to be seen. The Ruettiger house was one of a row of identical gray brick houses packed tightly next to one another. Like the other streets in Joliet, this one, too, was deserted. The action was inside the houses; most of the men and boys of Joliet were gathered in front of their television sets watching Notre Dame play Southern California.

Thirteen-year-old Rudy Ruettiger sat rigidly on the edge of his chair saying a silent prayer for his beloved Fighting Irish. Southern Cal was tough—"a formidable foe," as one of the announcers kept repeating to

Rudy's annoyance. Rudy had studied up on the Trojans. They had twenty-six lettermen left over from the
national champions who had beaten Wisconsin the
year before, 42–37, in one of the all-time great Rose
Bowl games. Hugh Devore, the new Notre Dame
coach, had installed Frank Budka at quarterback, injured ankle and all, and he seemed slow to Rudy, like
a truck toiling up a steep grade.

"Man, if we only still had Lamonica," he muttered,
pressing his fist hard against his knee. "Why did he
have to go and graduate?"

Rudy's eighteen-year-old brother, Frank, was
drinking a bottle of Falstaff and intently watching the
game. Their dad, Danilo, had kept up with the action
through most of the first quarter, yelling for the Irish
to step it up, to put a whipping on those California
fruitcakes, but by the half he had fallen asleep. How
could he? Rudy wondered. He knew that his father
and older brother loved Notre Dame football passionately, but it seemed pretty clear to him that they didn't
love it as passionately as he did. He stared at his father. How could anybody in his right mind fall asleep
during a Notre Dame game? It was insane. Maybe it
was even unpatriotic, Rudy thought. Although, he admitted, maybe it was all right for his brother Johnny
not to put his whole heart into the Irish. He was six-
teen, halfway in age between Rudy and Frank, and he
wasn't like the other Ruettiger males. All Johnny
cared about was art; he loved to draw pictures. He
could have been an athlete if he'd put his mind to it;
he had good physical coordination—better than mine,
Rudy sadly admitted to himself—but sports, especially spectator sports, meant nothing to him. While

the others sat glued to the TV for any sports that came on, including wrestling and bowling if there wasn't anything better, Johnny would stay up in his room, hunched over his desk making pictures.

When Southern Cal scored first and kicked the extra point, Rudy felt an ache growing in the pit of his stomach. Notre Dame had already lost to Wisconsin and Purdue—oh-and-two the first two games of the year—and with the talent Southern Cal was throwing at them, things definitely looked bad. Take Pete Beathard—man, he was some kind of quarterback! He was as good as there was. Rudy sent up a kind of prayer, if not directly to the Lord, at least to some higher force who might be willing to intervene in football matters. Please, he implored, I haven't been doing too good in school. I don't crack the books enough, I'm aware of that, but please give us this win and I'll make a bigger effort in the future. I really will. I'll try to get my grades up into the C range.

Rudy's pleading worked. The Irish broke loose and began to move the ball downfield. They got into Trojan territory, with Bill Wolski running for consistent short gains, and suddenly the score was 7-6, and then the placekick sailed over the crossbar and split the goalpost uprights neatly in two, and the score was tied.

"Great, *great,*" Rudy yelled, clapping his hands. "Way to go, Irish!"

"They got 'em on the run now," Frank said. He got up, belched, stretched, yawned, and slouched toward the kitchen for another beer. Mr. Ruettiger opened an eye.

"They score?"

"Yup, sure did," said Rudy.

"Good." Mr. Ruettiger closed his eyes and in a moment resumed his snoring.

Betty Ruettiger looked in from the kitchen, shook her head, and said to Rudy and Frank with a grin, "Your father, the sound machine."

The Trojans scored again, but the Irish came roaring back, and Rudy, a historian in his own right, thought of history—football history, the only kind that counted. One of the great upset games was brewing, Rudy could almost taste it. It was going to be like Notre Dame against Army in 1928, when the Irish were outclassed but Knute Rockne delivered his great inspirational speech and the Irish went on to win. It was going to be like Notre Dame in 1952 against mighty Oklahoma, one of the truly great teams, when the Irish gritted their way to a fabulous finish. Rudy had his Notre Dame history down cold; dates, names, and stats all filed away neatly in his brain. If only they taught football in school he would pull down straight A's, and end up valedictorian besides.

At halftime the score was 14–14, and when the second half got under way, Rudy was so nervous he asked Frank for a taste of his beer.

"Get lost, shrimp," said his gruff, selfish older brother.

The third period was a seesaw affair, a battle of wills, with neither team scoring. Real nail-biting time. Rudy's knuckles were white on the armrests as he urged his team on. He couldn't for the life of him understand why Frank didn't care about the Irish as much as he did; even more in a way because Frank knew football from playing it. He'd been a first-string, sixty-minute player on his high-school football team, starring on both defense and offense. He'd been a big wheel until he graduated a year ago, and Rudy felt kind of sad that things had changed for Frank. Changed in just twelve short months. Now he was working in the steel mill with the old man, and although he didn't seem to mind, Rudy minded for both of them. He could keep going to school, he could keep on playing football. He could aspire to something more than . . . this.

He snuck a look at his older brother, who was in the middle of a long gulp of beer. He was putting on weight—not the good weight-lifting kind but Jell-O-y fatty pudding weight. More and more each day he reminded Rudy of their father. They would both come home from work, grab a beer, turn on the TV, and tune out the rest of the world—him, Ma, conversation, everything. And Frank was beginning to get crabby like the old man—always out of sorts and bitching about something.

Rudy turned down the volume during the commercial. He always did it and it always got him in mild hot water.

"Hey, whadja do that for?" said Frank.

"Yeah," said Danilo, his eyes closed. "Leave the sound."

"But it's so stupid," said Rudy.

"No it ain't," said Frank. "*You're* stupid."

"I like that jingle," said Danilo. "It sells cars, ya know."

"I just don't see anything in commercials," said Rudy. "To me, they're phony."

"Bullshit," said Frank.

"Watch your language there, Frankie," said Danilo mildly. "The thing is," he said to Rudy, "no commercials, no money for the networks. And what that means is, no football games. No Cubs, no Blackhawks. That ain't a pretty picture, now is it?"

"So don't knock 'em, little bro," said Frank, draining his beer. "You want another, Pop?" he said to Danilo as he rose and flexed his biceps. Rudy noticed that Frank's belly was beginning to flop over his belt. He wouldn't touch a salad on a bet.

"Sure, if you're headed for the kitchen."

Same old conversation, if you could call it conversation; it never varied and it got under Rudy's skin, though he tried not to let it. He loved his father and his brother—more, he sometimes suspected, than they loved him. And he made a mighty effort to understand them; he considered it his duty, like going to school and attending mass and never lying to Ma.

He turned the volume back up. The Trojans were using two elevens and the Irish were substituting by individuals. Rudy noticed the little things, the nuances; he took quiet pride in his knowledge of the game and the strategies the coaches employed. Southern Cal controlled the ball for most of the third period, and that worried Rudy. They were wearing Notre Dame down just as Wisconsin and Purdue had worn them down the previous two Saturdays; he just prayed that the fourth quarter wouldn't turn seriously gruesome. The last play of the third quarter practically gave Rudy a heart attack—a Trojan man shook his defender and crossed right under the goalpost, all alone, arms outstretched, the ball spiraling toward him mean and hard—one of those deadly Pete Beathard passes—the receiver seemed to stand high on the air waiting for the ball—but he dropped it, it had come in too low, around his ankles.

"Whew!" Rudy said out loud, and mopped his brow.

Rudy loved the Fighting Irish unconditionally; they could do no wrong. When they lost, there was a good reason, and when they won, they deserved to win. Rudy loved the University of Notre Dame almost as much as its football team. He'd read up on it; he knew its history—if not as completely as the football team, at least pretty completely. He was convinced that no Harvard or Yale or Princeton could compare either academically or athletically with the great Notre Dame, the realized dream of the French priest Father Sorin. Rudy had plowed through an article about the origins of the school (reading didn't come easily to him, but when the subject was Notre Dame or Irish football, he always made the effort). Back in November of 1842 Father Sorin set out with seven brothers and an oxcart to a tract of nine hundred acres near South Bend, where they would build the University of Notre Dame du Lac. The group made the two-hundred-and-fifty-mile trek from Vincennes, Indiana, to the spot where the construction would commence; they knelt in the snow, dedicated their work to Notre Dame (Our Lady), made bricks pale gold in color from the marl beds of the two lakes on the property, and talked the townspeople into helping with their noble enterprise.

The first students were sons of farmers, trappers, and merchants, and the concept was to keep students too busy to get into mischief. For one hundred dollars Father Sorin pledged to feed a student, wash and

mend his clothes, provide medical attention, and teach
the total curriculum—English, spelling, reading,
grammar, history, astronomy, and surveying. If a parent couldn't pay in cash, Father Sorin would take payment in grain, furniture, or farm animals. If you
wanted to take a special elective like Latin and the
family couldn't pay in cash, a plump pig could ensure
the student a place in the classroom.

Notre Dame was Father Sorin's dream, and Rudy
also had his dream—a dream he'd managed so far to
hold tight to himself; not even Ma could be allowed
in to share it just yet. No Ruettiger had ever advanced
beyond a high-school degree, but Rudy was determined to put an end to that sorry record. And not just
any old college would do, either. He had his heart set
on Notre Dame. And that was only part of the dream,
and maybe not even the biggest part. One day—somehow, someway, if only for one down—he was going
to wear the blue-and-gold uniform of the Notre Dame
football team. He could just hear Frank laughing at his
dream, the mocking laughter, and could imagine his
brother's exact words: "Yeah, sure, little bro. Here
you are, a five-feet-four, one-hundred-pound bag of
nothin', you ain't all that coordinated, and you ain't
exactly a rocket scientist, either. Wake up, little
brother. Get yourself a little whiff of reality." That
was pretty much what Rudy could expect from Frank,
and it wouldn't be any better from his old man. Danilo
would want him to go into the steel mill the morning
after he got his high-school diploma and start bringing
in some money. Dreams were for other people, not the
likes of the Ruettigers. But why should he limit his
dreams and bow to their idea of reality? Somehow,

someway . . . he didn't know exactly how or when, but he would make it happen. He would arrive in South Bend, luggage in hand, ready to start his real life.

Rudy's face was now inches from the TV screen. Good things were unfolding for the Irish, magical things. Budka was coming through consistently now on third-down situations. He got one first down himself on a bootleg play; he must be smelling blood and victory, Rudy thought, because he was moving much more quickly now—charged up, alert—as he faked the handoff to the back going around the end of the line to the left and he took off with the ball to the right. Six precious yards! A great call, that bootleg! Go, man, go! More often than not, though, Budka got the Irish their first down by a matter of inches. He was grinding it out, inching the team downfield; the team was going for every inch of turf, every block, every tackle, and it was working, and Rudy was beside himself with joy—joy mixed with panic. After all, they could still lose. Still break his heart.

The Trojans stopped Notre Dame's drive deep in their own territory, but the Irish turned right around and stopped the Trojans, blocking off Garrett's speed, rushing Beathard's passes, even sacking him twice. The Notre Dame defensive line, in a frenzy of pursuit, was forcing Beathard into hurrying his passes. The haste was ruining his accuracy, and even when his passes seemed on the money, the Irish defenders were shadowing their men like a second skin and batting the ball away.

"I'll do my homework every night," Rudy prayed. "I'll pass all my subjects. I'll stay awake in class."

With the final period more than half-gone, Rudy dared to hope for the first time with his whole heart. He knew how dangerous that was because if the Irish lost now, with his whole entire heart on the line, he'd cry all night. He wouldn't get any sleep at all. But it wasn't going to happen! The Trojans had lost their poise, their confidence and execution. You could see it in their slumped postures, their glum expressions. And with less than two minutes to go, Notre Dame had possession. Two yards on a fullback dive right up the middle. Just plain muscle, no deception. Four yards on a draw play, beautifully executed by a fired-up Budka. And now they were within field-goal range. With less than six minutes left in the game, Ken Ivan came in and calmly kicked what proved to be the winning field goal.

Score: Notre Dame 17—Southern California 14.

A miracle.

Rudy, whistling the Irish fight song, ran upstairs to his room, opened his science book, and buried his face in it. After a moment he looked up at the ceiling.

"Thank you," he said. And then burst out in a loud voice full of adolescent cracks: *"Cheer, cheer for old Notre Dame. Wake up the echoes, cheering her name. . . ."*

2

Late that afternoon, once the Notre Dame–Southern Cal showdown was over and the announcers had milked the game for every last piece of analysis, Rudy, Frank, and Johnny joined a group of teenage boys for a game of touch football on a hard-packed dirt lot a few blocks from the Ruettiger house. Tufts of dirty green grass that hugged a rusted cross-wire fence surrounding the lot were the only signs of color; the sun was low in the sky over Joliet and the dim day was growing dimmer, grayer by the minute. But the colors in Rudy's mind were neither dim nor gray. He was still riding the bright high of the Irish win that afternoon; he had already played the highlights over in his mind, and he had effortlessly inserted himself as one of the Notre Dame stars. He had a vision of himself taking the hike from center, fading back à la Budka, and looking for a free receiver, setting himself in the pocket and heaving a bomb—perfect arc, beau-

tiful spiral—touchdown! Fifty yards! Roars for Rudy
Ruettiger, a.k.a. the Joliet Flash, from the packed
stands!

The only trouble was, he wasn't the quarterback,
not even in this puny pickup game; he was the center,
one of the soldiers in the trenches. Last one to be
picked—as always—and, in his opinion, stuck with
the worst possible position.

"I'm tired of being center," he complained to
Frank.

"C'mon, little bro. You're lucky to even be out
here. So eat dirt and like it."

Rudy strapped his battered gold helmet under his
chin. He was the only kid with a helmet; he'd bought
it the year before with money he'd made selling *Life,
Look,* and *Collier's* door-to-door. He leaned over the
ball, knees bent, getting ready to hike. He wondered
why Frank had to be such a mean bastard. He wondered if mean older brothers were the norm the world
over—although Johnny wasn't mean, at least most of
the time. But then Johnny was kind of strange, not
like other kids.

Just as Rudy was about to hike he stood up and
said, "Anybody want to wear my helmet? I'll switch
positions with you."

Eddie Pinto shook his head and started to walk
away. "I'm s'posed to be jerkin' sodas. It's almost
seven."

"Old Ed eats as many sodas as he makes," said one
of the boys, slapping another boy on the back and
showing off his braces in a big grin.

"Hey, Eddie, my man," said Frank. "Not in the

middle of the freakin' game. I mean we got a tie score here, know what I mean?"

"I gotta go, Frank. I'm not shittin' ya. I really do."

"Don't leave, buddy. We need you."

"Yeah, man," said Rudy, trying to make his voice low and tough like Frank's.

"Shut up," said Frank without glancing in his direction.

"I can't be late for work," said Eddie. "The boss is already on my ass."

"C'mon—one more score."

Eddie looked tempted but then shook his head. "Let Rudy play in my place."

"Yeah, Frank," said Johnny, "good thought. Let Rudy fill in for Eddie."

"No way," said Frank.

But when more of the players started to drift off, Frank realized he'd have to give in or the game would be over. And Frank loved to play football, even in a rinky-dink, pickup scrub game like this with younger guys most of whom couldn't carry his jersey in terms of talent. When Frank was in action he felt alive, once again the high-school hero, one of the truly blessed. When he was in the middle of the play—running, passing, laying on a hard cross-body block—he could forget about the steel mill and the impending marriage to Melinda and about the kids they were bound to have, one after another, a bunch of them according to Melinda, and concentrate on what he loved the most. On what made him feel alive and at one with himself.

"Okay," he said to Rudy reluctantly. "You can rush the passer."

"Great," Rudy said with a large, happy grin. "That's great, Frank."

Johnny picked up the ball and tossed it up and down in his hands. "It's getting dark," he said. "We should shag it for home. Besides, Frank, Ma gets pissed when we're late for supper."

"But it's a tie game," Rudy said.

"Yeah, what's the hurry, Johnny, huh?" Frank gave him a not-so-gentle poke in the ribs. "Your next Michelangelo or what the hell can wait awhile. Give it a rest, why don'tcha."

"You can't hardly see your hand in front of your face."

"Whoever scores first wins," said Frank to the others, ignoring Johnny. "How's that grab you guys?"

"It better be fast," Johnny said.

Frank flipped a coin, calling it in the air. "Heads," he said. "Our ball."

As the players took their positions Rudy got down in a three-point stance, his body weight resting on the balls of his feet, his right hand on the ground for proper balance, his head up so that he could read the defense—just as he had studied it so many times from the diagrams in the football guidebook he'd bought years ago, now dog-eared from constant use.

"Take that stupid helmet off," Frank told him. "We're Notre Dame, you're Navy."

Rudy didn't move as he looked across the line of scrimmage at his older brother. He wanted to shout that *he* was the one who had every right to be Notre Dame, that *he* was more loyal to the Irish than anyone, but he realized how childish that would sound and could already hear the barrage of abuse he'd get for saying it.

"Remember," Frank said to Pete Sturges, "I'm Frank Budka, you're Bill Wolski—and hey, Rudy, you're some dumb midshipman. Take your pick. They all stink."

"Oh sure, right," said Rudy. "They only ranked number two in the nation. And I guess Roger Staubach stinks."

"I say they stink, little bro. So they stink."

The ball was hiked to Frank, and Rudy charged as Frank backpedaled, looking down the dusky lot for a receiver. Rudy lunged, stumbled, just missing Frank, who did a neat feint to his left.

"Get him, Rudy. Get him!" Johnny yelled.

Rudy dove flat out, trying desperately to tag Frank, but with a grin and a head fake, Frank niftily dodged him again. Rudy, clutching air with his hands, lost his balance and sprawled out face-first in the dirt. Stepping forward around his younger brother's body, Frank spiraled a beautiful pass downfield, right into the outstretched arms of Pete Sturges.

"Budka to Wolski," Frank yelled, shaking his fists at the dark sky. "Touchdown! The Irish win again!"

He shook Pete's hand and slapped some of his other teammates on the back. Rudy was still spread-eagled on the ground, cursing to himself. Frank looked down at him and laughed. "Jesus, what a spaz," he said.

"Lay off him, Frank," said Johnny.

Frank wagged a finger in Johnny's face and said, "So now we hear from the great arteest—God's gift to the world of painting. Well, you're a spaz, too,

Johnny boy. Whataya think of that? You should draw yourself in motion. You'd split a gut laughing."

Without replying, Johnny helped Rudy to his feet.

"That was some terrific pass, Frankie," Rudy said. As badly as he wanted to keep his mouth shut, Rudy couldn't help complimenting his brother. There was just no way he could stay mad at Frank, not with all of Frank's inborn talent, his natural sense of physical grace. And there was something else. Rudy sensed that behind all the bluster and the tough-guy ways, his older brother was a very fragile human being. Rudy couldn't stand the thought of hurting him. He felt that if he saw Frank broken—stripped of his defenses, his hard shell, his wiseguy exterior—he would die of shame and pity.

Frank led the guys in a race down the dark and barren streets, dropping them off one at a time at their homes. Rudy lagged behind, kicking a pebble along the sidewalk, hating for the day to end. Because tomorrow was Sunday and that meant the next day would be Monday. School. Stupid subjects that had nothing to do with his life. Dull teachers with dull minds and rotten tempers. If only he could go to sleep and wake up, not in the eighth grade but in his freshman year of college—in South Bend. The subjects and the teachers would be a lot more challenging; he would make the football team, proudly wearing the blue and gold, there would be terrific friendships, and the world would be his. Not like here in old Joliet, the armpit of the universe.

He watched Frank, Johnny, and Pete Sturges cut left and bound up the stairs of his house. They all removed their shoes at the front door—standing orders of Ma's after any outdoors activity. Rudy slouched in a minute after the others. Food was set out on the table, buffet style—meat loaf, mashed potatoes, hot rolls, ears of hot buttered corn, broccoli fried and smothered in cheese, the only way anyone in the family would eat it. The TV was on with the sound low (it was on steadily from morning until bedtime on weekends) and no one was watching it.

Danilo waved an ear of corn at the boys. "Hey, Pete, you got a home of your own?" Rudy noticed that his father's face had turned about four beers redder than when they'd left to play ball.

"Yes, sir," said Pete. "Last time I looked."

Everybody laughed.

"You're welcome here anytime," said Betty.

Rudy was pained to see that Sherry Wolinski had come by and was fixing herself a plate of food. She was a few months older than Rudy, and in his homeroom and most of his classes. Although she and Rudy were wearing each other's class rings and she was a pretty girl, with curly brunette hair and an hourglass figure, and even though she generously helped him with his homework, which he was too busy dreaming to do, Rudy felt a little uncomfortable when she came around on the spur of the moment like this. She lived just a block and a half down the street, so it was kind of natural to drop in without calling; still, he didn't like it. He'd have to talk to her about the importance of having some privacy once in a while. All of their school friends knew they were going steady, and every so often Sherry even talked about the future when they would settle down and get married and all.

That sort of talk made Rudy extremely nervous. After all, they were only thirteen. He wasn't ready to even think about stuff like that. As far as he was concerned, that was a future beyond the future, somewhere out there in space.

Danilo, winking at Frank, turned to Sherry and said, "Now tell me, young lady, who are you again?"

It was the same old stupid routine, and Rudy hated it with a passion. That was another reason he didn't like her dropping in without an invitation. Frank and the old man always ended up making fun of her. And the worst part about that was she didn't seem to have a clue. She was a sweet girl with a good heart, but she wasn't too quick on the uptake when it came to humor and sarcasm; it just went over her head. She was a hardworking, honor-roll student, but when it came to understanding what life was all about, she struck Rudy as kind of backward.

"*You* know who I am," she said, giggling. "I'm Sherry Wolinski."

Danilo nodded. "Oh yes, Bob Wolinski's kid."

"Rudy's girlfriend." Frank nodded. "His heart-throb. His one and only. The passion of his life."

"Ah, come on, Frank," Rudy said, "will ya knock it off with that stuff?" He wished for one guilty moment that everybody in the room—with the possible exception of Ma and maybe Johnny on a good day—would instantly vaporize.

"Well, it's true," Sherry said, smiling shyly in Rudy's direction. A very pretty smile, he had to admit. "I am your girl."

He gave her a sickly smile.

"I'm always going to be your girl," she pronounced, and moved next to Rudy and took his hand in hers.

Everybody started grinning and laughing—even Ma and Johnny, usually his allies—and that drove Rudy crazy. But he wouldn't let them know it; no way would he give them that satisfaction. Gently he withdrew his hand from Sherry's and moved to the buffet table for a plate, even though he'd completely lost his appetite.

"So, Frankie," said Danilo, "how are the Hilltoppers gonna do tomorrow night?"

"That's an easy one, Pop. They're gonna kick ass."

"Watch your language, Frank," said Betty, rolling her eyes apologetically at Sherry.

"Coach Gillespie said Frank was the best athlete on the Hilltoppers," Rudy told Sherry. He was stretching the truth a little, but Frank *had* been a star at Joliet Catholic, especially in his junior year when he led the team in yardage gained. For some reason, he slacked off in his senior year and didn't start the last two games of the season.

"The team ain't the same without him this year," said Danilo. He took a long tug on his beer. "The good Lord don't make many like Frankie here."

"The Hilltoppers are still damn good," said Frank.

"Please, son," said Betty. "Set an example. Swearing shows a—"

"—limited vocabulary," Frank and Rudy chimed in.

Everyone laughed, even Betty.

"Frank almost made All-Conference in his junior year," said Rudy, hoping to impress on Sherry that there was much more to Frank than met the eye.

" 'Almost' only counts in horseshoes," said Frank with a dismissive wave of his hand.

"I think I saw you play," Sherry said. She smiled at him.

"If you'd seen me, you'd remember," said Frank, smirking.

"Well, we're not at all conceited, are we?" said Sherry, and Rudy couldn't help grinning. He loved her for that sudden show of spirit, especially standing up to Frank, who had a way of shrinking people practically to invisibility.

"We're all going to the Hilltoppers game tomorrow night," Danilo said.

"Not me," said Betty. "You can count me out."

"Well, I didn't mean you, Mother," said Danilo.

"You mean I'm not part of 'we all'?" she said with mock anger, hands on hips.

"*You* know what I mean," he said irritably, stabbing with his fork for another ear of corn.

Johnny, the quiet member of the family, raised his hand. Danilo stared at him. His middle son perplexed him more than the other two combined. He never knew what the boy was thinking or feeling, and when Johnny did say something, it usually made Danilo angry or else confused him. "What is it, John?" he said. "We ain't in school here. No need to raise your hand. If you got somethin' to say, just interrupt like everybody else."

Johnny moved his mashed potatoes around on his plate as he said, "Joliet Junior College has some art classes next summer for high school." There was a sudden silence in the room; he paused, stared angrily at his potatoes, and then raced on. "They're really supposed to be terrific and they ain't that expensive—that's what I heard from this guy who was in the program last year. It's a real—like an opportunity and all? I really want to do it."

Silence.

Then Danilo said slowly, "Art classes? What is this? You gonna make a living as some artist?"

"Along with all the other fruits," said Frank.

"Shut up, Frankie," said Danilo. "This is serious." To Johnny he said, "Well? Is this what you figure you're gonna do with your life?"

Johnny shrugged, blushed, and burned a hole in his father's face with a quick glance. "Maybe."

"Maybe not," Frank said.

"Stay out of it," Johnny said.

"Stay out of what?" Frank said innocently.

There was no humor in Johnny's smile as he said, "Are you planning to make a living as a football player? You got that goal all worked out, Frank?"

"If I feel like it." Frank looked flustered. For years he had talked about going directly from high school to the pros, but there had been little interest—possibly because of his lack of size and relative lack of speed, and maybe because what interest there was he'd never pursued—and as expected, he had followed his father into the mill.

Danilo said to Johnny, "What you got lined up next summer is something solid, something you can depend on."

"I know. A job at the mill."

"Don't knock it," said Frank.

"Put a lid on it, Frankie," said Danilo. "This is between me and Johnny." He leaned forward across the table toward Johnny, his stomach pushing against the table, his face flushed even deeper, and there was an edge to his voice. "You're gonna make more money than any of your classmates. Is that such a bad thing?"

"I know the money's good, but—"

"It's a damn good company and a damn good job. It's managed to keep all a you fed and clothed all these years."

Johnny dropped his head, trying to avoid his father's growing fury. "I know that's true. I just don't want to work there, okay?"

Then don't, Rudy's mind screamed out. *Do what you feel you have to do and to hell with everything else!*

Danilo's voice was beginning to tremble; it was all he could do to keep his temper in check.

"Go find a job where you can make more than five bucks an hour, where you have union protection, and relations to look out for your front and back sides. If you have such good fortune, then God be with you."

"But, Pop, I want to take those art courses. That's what I want more than anything. Didn't you ever want something really bad? Can't you understand?" He snuck a look at his father, got caught by his inflamed eyes, and quickly looked away.

Danilo struck the table with the flat of his hand. Plates rattled. "Get out of my sight," he shouted. "You give me indigestion. You make me want to puke."

"Let the boy alone," said Betty, putting a restraining hand on Danilo's shoulder. He shrugged it off.

"Mr. Smartass can make his own way," Danilo said. "Just listen. The arrogant little bastard thinks he can get through life without doing an honest day's work for an honest day's pay. Well, he ain't gonna use *me* as a welfare department—"

"Danilo, please . . ."

He waved his wife's words away. Sherry began to sniffle.

"You'd better stop all this dreamin'," he said to Johnny. "You hear me?"

Johnny shook his head and stood. "I'd rather not eat," he said. "This is your food." He threw his napkin on the table and stalked out of the room.

Danilo lurched over to the refrigerator and pulled out another bottle of Falstaff.

"You've had enough," said Betty.

"Yeah, Pop," said Rudy. "Take it easy."

"I've had enough of all of you, that's what I've had," said Danilo. "You all like to tell me what you're gonna do and you don't listen when I speak." He gave the air a fierce karate chop. "I am the head of this family *and I will be respected.*"

Frank nodded his head. "Damn right," he muttered.

Danilo swung his head back and forth, his eyes red and bleary, not entirely focused. "Now, does anybody else here have anything to say?"

"I'm starting the dishes," said Betty. "Please keep your voice down."

"I'll help you, Mrs. Ruettiger," said Sherry, gathering up some dirty plates and quickly heading for the kitchen.

Rudy raised his hand, wondering why he was doing the very thing that would displease his father. Danilo slowly shook his head and whispered something Rudy couldn't hear. "What's with all this schoolroom crap?" he said.

"Just trying to be polite."

"So whataya got to say?"

Rudy cleared his throat, took a deep breath, and said, "After high school I'm going to college."

"You're going to college," Danilo repeated.

"Yeah. Not just any old college, either. Notre Dame."

Rudy had been keeping this news to himself for longer than he could remember, but Johnny's courage to lay his dream on the line had triggered something in him. He knew he couldn't have picked a worse moment, with his old man already so hot under the collar. He tried to bite his tongue and wait for a better time to spring it on Danilo, but it was almost as though he had no choice in the matter. If he didn't speak up now, he didn't know if he'd ever summon up the nerve again.

Danilo's beer was halfway to his mouth and it stayed there. He looked at his youngest son as though he had just said he was flying to the moon first thing in the morning.

Frank reached over and cuffed Rudy alongside the head. "Sure, and I'm gonna buy a mansion on Lake Shore Drive. Along with a Rolls and a Jag. And marry Miss Illinois while I'm at it."

Pete started giggling and Danilo allowed himself a tight smile. "Notre Dame, eh?" he said. "What are you, twelve? Thirteen?"

"You know I'm thirteen."

"The eighth grade, right?"

"Eighth grade, Pop. You've got it right."

"What are you, a D student, just scrapin' by? A chip off the old block, you might say?"

"Low C," said Rudy, avoiding everybody's eye.

"Most of my classes are stupid. They teach a lot of boring junk."

"Never in my family or your ma's has anybody gone to college. I'm not against college, I got nothin' against higher education, but for crissake, boy, you can't even cut it in junior high. You're just like your brother Johnny—you think dreams are more real than life. All I can tell you is, you better wake up and smell the coffee before it's too late."

Rudy walked Sherry home, declined an offer of hot chocolate and homemade pound cake, and walked back to his house, kicking a pebble all the way. He knew his old man was right; he *was* a lousy student. But he also knew Danilo was wrong. Without dreams there was no purpose to life, nothing to drive you on to greater effort and the chance of true fulfillment. Without goals to reach for, you might as well be a house dog or a cow out in the pasture sleeping and eating your whole life away. Each day like the one before with nothing new to look forward to. Thomas Edison had dreams; Henry Ford had dreams; Marconi had dreams—yes, and Knute Rockne had dreams. . . .

In the bedroom he shared with Johnny and Frank, with the door closed, Rudy dropped a 45 down a spindle onto a small record player. He put the needle in the groove and sat back on his bunk bed to listen as he had so many hundreds of times before. Above his bed was a Notre Dame pennant and pictures of many of the fabled players past and present—George Gipp, the Four Horsemen, Johnny Lujack, Paul Hornung, Bronco Nagurski, Daryle Lamonica, and dozens of others.

We're going inside of 'em, came the scratchy voice of Knute Rockne, worn by constant replaying. *We're going outside of 'em—and when we get 'em on the run once, we're going to beat 'em on the run. . . .*

Rudy mouthed the words along with Rockne, his face intense, his fists beating on the bed in rhythm with the words.

Frank shoved the door open and barged into the room. He was holding a record of his own. "The new Elvis," he announced in a loud voice. "Let's give it a listen." He walked up to the record player and started to pull the needle off. Rudy shot up from the bed and stood between the record player and his much bigger older brother.

"It's the Rockne speech," Rudy said. "C'mon, Frank, please. Elvis can wait."

"Hey, little bro, you know the stupid speech by heart," Frank said.

But as he listened to Rockne's voice, its passionate rise and fall, the sincerity of the words, Frank's expression softened. He, too, shared Rudy's love of the Irish, although now that he was a workingman beginning to make his own way in the world, he tried to bury his boyish enthusiasms beneath a tough exterior.

He sat down on the bed beside Rudy and ruffled his younger brother's hair. Together, they listened.

. . . We're going to go, go, go, and we aren't going to stop until we go over the goal line. Today is the day we're going to win. They can't lick us. What do you say men?

There was the sound of players roaring as they charged out of the locker room—the very room, Rudy vowed, he would one day come charging out of wearing the blue-and-gold uniform so rich in tradition and glorious history.

PART

TWO

☆

1968

3

Dust motes danced in the bars of sun pouring in through the window. It was a lazy warm October afternoon and Rudy found it almost impossible to concentrate on rules of law in the distant past. Who cared? What did it have to do with his life? What did it have to say about Ma's arthritis or the old man's weight problem or whether you could work in the mill year after year without losing your sensitivity and any sense of reality? Father Ted, a soft-spoken gray-haired civics instructor with a sly sense of humor (rare in a teacher, Rudy thought) was using a pointer and a wall chart as he delivered his lecture. "The bicameral legislature originated not in England but where?"

Father Ted turned toward the class and immediately spotted Rudy staring out the window. Pete Sturges, sitting by Rudy's side, cleared his throat in an obvious attempt to get his friend's attention. Sherry, who sat directly in front of Rudy, smiled into her lap and shook her head as though to say, "He *is* my boyfriend but I won't put any bets on his sanity." The priest, with a little smile of his own, walked over and stood directly in front of Rudy, but Rudy's mind was all wrapped up in a fantasy and not available to mere teachers.

Ara Parseghian throws his arm around my shoulder and says, "Glad to have you here at Notre Dame, Rudy. The Irish really need a great running back, and with your speed and instincts, you really fill the bill. I know you have a little financial problem, we're all well aware of your situation, but don't you worry about that. A boy like you we make room for here at Notre Dame. There are scholarships, there's plenty of expert tutorial help. All we ask is that you apply yourself on the field and off, and I can promise you the best four years of your life. . . . "

Sherry stretched her leg back as far as she could and tried to make contact with Rudy's foot.

"Mr. Ruettiger," said Father Ted, "would you be interested in joining us? I'm sure you're having a far better time wherever you are, but your presence in class would be appreciated."

Some of the girls in class tittered and Rudy looked up, startled. "What?"

"The bicameral legislature didn't originate in England. Where did it originate?"

"Where?"

"That's the question, Mr. Ruettiger—for you to answer, not me."

"Yes . . . Yes. Bicameral. The bicameral legislature. Something about the Senate, the House of Representatives—right?'' Rudy began to stutter as he tried to pull his thoughts together.

Father Ted clucked his tongue. "Don't even try. If I were giving grades for dreaming, you would be getting straight A's. You would be all-honors. But alas, here in boring old civics, you're failing.'' Father Ted glanced around at the others in the class, his expression, with some extra intent in it, resting on Sherry Wolinski. "The problem with dreamers is they aren't doers. Unless they make sure their dreams have some practical application, they often become underachievers. Their accomplishments are outstanding up here"—he pointed to Rudy's head—"but here where it counts"—he picked up Rudy's notebook, opened it, leafed through the empty pages, shook his head, and sighed—"they always tend to come up short.''

Rudy suddenly hated the priest's smile. The man was definitely insincere, a phony—pleasant on the outside but secretly mean and always happy to give you a kick when you were down, aimed at the most vulnerable spot. Just like most teachers. The grade was what counted, nothing else. They didn't care about your character, they didn't give a damn about your true feelings and your ambitions. To them you were a grade—A, B, C, D, or Fail.

With his smile firmly in place, Father Ted dropped the notebook on Rudy's desk. The other students stared at Rudy, some with the sympathy you show the victim of a car wreck, but others with smirky superior grins.

The bell rang. The class started to rise.

"Hold up," said Father Ted, raising his hand, palm out, like a school guard directing traffic. "I have an announcement here." He picked up a sheet of paper from his desk, adjusted his rimless glasses higher on his nose, and started reading. "If you are a student interested in making the University of Notre Dame your college choice, a bus will be waiting for you on Saturday, November fifteenth, at ten A.M. for a one-day guided tour of the campus, its facilities, and the educational opportunities offered by this great institution of higher learning. Only serious students are welcome. Please sign up by Wednesday, November fifth. Class dismissed."

Rudy gathered up his stuff, his perpetual schoolroom scowl dissolving into a grin. Those were the words he had been waiting to hear for years, had been dreaming about and planning for. In three weeks he would travel to South Bend and he would lay eyes on Notre Dame for the first time. His heart began to race at the thought.

Pete and Sherry joined him in the hall outside of class.

"Great move—*Mr. Ruettiger*—falling asleep in class," said Pete. "That's bound to win you plenty of brownie points with Father Fruitcake. You're really somethin' else."

"I wasn't asleep," said Rudy. "I was thinking."

"About me, no doubt," said Sherry, linking her arm in his.

"Sure," he said. "Hey, Pete, you takin' the South Bend tour?"

"You betcha," Pete answered. "I prob'ly don't stand a chance of gettin' in, but why not go look the deal over? I've been on the honor roll all semester. Not a single C. But my folks can't afford to send me around the corner for beer and pretzels, much less to that place." He nudged Sherry's arm and said to Rudy, "And what are you gonna do on the fifteenth? Sit up in your room listening to that old Knute Rockne rah-rah speech?"

"Very funny, Sturges."

"You're not thinkin' of going to South Bend, are you?"

Rudy started to answer—started to tell the truth, that he was planning to sign up for the trip, regardless of a report card liberally sprinkled with C's and D's, along with the inevitable failing grade in civics—but then he saw Sherry staring at him, saw the sadness in her expression, and decided to say nothing. They didn't believe in him any more than Father Ted did, and they were his two best friends.

"We've got the chemistry exam on Thursday," Sherry said. "You wanna come over and cram with me, Rudy?" That was her tactful translation of: "Would you like to come over and study my notes?"

She expected his automatic response—"No, I've got some things to do"—but he surprised her. "Yeah," he said instead, "I guess that would be a good idea. I've gotten kinda behind. I'd better polish up a little on those old carbon chains." It was the first time in a month he had agreed to study with her after school.

As they walked home, Rudy and Pete tossed a football back and forth—one would run a pattern and the other would do the passing. Sherry carried their books. When they got to Pete's house, Rudy said, "So you're really gonna go on the trip?"

"Yeah. Nothin' to lose."

"Would you like to go to Notre Dame? I mean would you really like to go there more than anything?"

Pete shrugged. "I'm not sure I'm college material. I've been looking at some stuff about the navy. I might join up."

"You're college material if you think you are," said Rudy.

"Maybe. I don't know. Maybe I don't think I am."

Rudy nodded, started to say something, then changed his mind. "Take 'er easy, Pete. See you tomorrow in prison."

"Bye, Pete," said Sherry, and she and Rudy walked on. She chatted about this and that, but Rudy was uncharacteristically quiet. She glanced at him, reached for his hand. "Anything wrong?"

"No."

"Did Father Ted get under your skin?"

"I'm okay."

She squeezed his hand and said, "You're going on that trip to South Bend, aren't you? I can tell you are. You've got that certain look in your eye, that faraway look."

He snuck a look at her profile. "Would you think I'm crazy if I did go?"

"No. I know what it means to you."

He stopped and turned to her. "You promise not to say anything to Pete or anybody else?"

"Promise." She placed her hand on her heart.

"The answer is yes. You couldn't keep me away with machine guns." He looked to see if they were being watched, and when he was satisfied they were alone, he leaned forward and kissed her on the lips.

"You think I'm crazy, don't you?"

"No, Rudy. I love you."

"Well, maybe I am crazy. But who cares?"

At eighteen, Rudy's body had filled out nicely but had refused to sprout up. He seemed destined to be stuck at five feet six inches, forever looking up at others. In the high-school weight room he would try to stretch himself by hanging from the chin-up bar until his arm sockets were on fire, but so far he hadn't added a fraction of an inch to his stature. As he studied himself critically in the bathroom mirror (a preoccupation indulged in at every available opportunity during his teen years), he approved of his upper body buildup as much as he loathed his shortness. To compensate for his lack of size and poor academic performance, he went out for every sport at Joliet Catholic. He excelled in wrestling—an individual sport in which guts and determination mattered almost as much as inborn physical skills. He made the varsity football team in his junior year, but played very little except for special teams. The problem was, his teammates were growing and he wasn't.

At home, things were not too terrific, which was another reason for making his Notre Dame dream come true. As each month brought him closer to graduating from high school, Danilo harped more and more on the advantages of going to work in the mill—union protection, good wages, lifetime friendships, a great pension down the line. "You go to work at eighteen," Danilo had told him not once but dozens of times, "by forty-eight you got your thirty years in. The big pension kicks in. You're sittin' on the fat of the land and you still got your whole life ahead of you. Now, how can you beat that?'' By living a life, Rudy wanted to yell at him. By doing something that gives you satisfaction and a sense of pride. The old man's arguments fell on deaf ears, just as they had for so long with Johnny. And yet how had Johnny ended up? Twenty years old now, dating that stupid Dolores Kearns, working in the mill just like Frank and the old man and still living at home. And no more talk of being an artist. For crissake, twenty years old, and as far as Rudy could see, his brother's life was over. Rudy wouldn't—he couldn't—let the same thing happen to him. There was simply no way he would let Danilo dictate the terms of life to him.

So there was a lot of tension at home, a lot of arguments and raised voices. Ma spent too much time playing the role of referee as her men battled away, and Rudy found himself spending more and more of his time at the Wolinski house. Lately he had practically been living there. Mr. and Mrs. Wolinski respected him. They listened to him without interrupting. They treated him like an adult. But his relationship with Sherry did present problems. She was planning on their getting married as soon as they graduated in June, and Rudy just couldn't see fencing himself in that way. Then there would be no Notre Dame, no life, an end to his dreams; instead, there would be the mill, a bunch of kids, beer hangovers, and an expanding waistline like Frank's and Danilo's (at least Johnny was managing to stay in shape). When Rudy thought of being stuck in Joliet all his life, he wondered if he wouldn't be better off dead. Not that he didn't love Sherry—he really did. She was pretty, she was sexy, she could talk to all kinds of people and get along with them, and socially she wasn't a slob like Johnny's girl. She knew which side of the plate the fork belonged on. But marriage? There was no way he could take that step—not now, not for a long time— and he knew he risked losing her if he kept stalling.

The good moments at the Ruettiger house these days were those times when they all watched sports together—especially football and most especially Notre Dame football. On a Saturday in early November, Danilo, Frank, Pete, and Rudy sat huddled around the TV set. Johnny was present, too, but lying on the floor enveloped in a cloud of cigar smoke. "Coley O'Brien fades back to pass," shouted the announcer. "He looks downfield, he throws. Gladieux's got it! He's got it! Thirty, twenty, fifteen, ten, five—*touchdown!*"

Rudy jumped in the air, screaming and clapping his hands. Pete, grinning, gave Rudy a thumbs-up sign. Frank sat in the corner in his work clothes, his fists clenched, a tight grin creasing his cheeks.

"Let's go, Irish!" Rudy yelled. "National champions!"

Sitting in his familiar chair and nearly overflowing it with his bulk, Danilo raised a cautionary hand. "Settle down," he said. "It ain't over yet."

Johnny rolled over, yawned, and looked up at Rudy pumping his fist. "Does it mean that much to you?" he said softly.

Everyone stared at Johnny.

Rudy broke the silence, saying, "I'd give my right arm to be out there on that field."

"Yeah," Frank said, laughing, "the Irish would

sure have to be hard up. Recruiting one-armed players with D averages."

"C-minus," said Rudy quickly. To Johnny he said, "I'm going to be a student at Notre Dame one day—and I'll be on that field in the blue-and-gold uniform. I know none of you believe me, you all think it's a stupid pipe dream, but I tell you it's gonna happen."

Frank laughed louder. "You're a madman, you know that? You're nuts."

Johnny studied Rudy through a thick cloud of smoke but said nothing.

"Quiet, all a you," said Danilo. "The game's not over."

Frank, speaking more softly, said, "Your buddy Pete here lives and breathes the Cubs. Right, Petey?"

"You bet, Frank."

"But we don't have to hear all the time about how he's gonna be their next shortstop."

"It's different," Rudy said.

"Yeah, right," said Frank. He sighed, and grabbed his lunch pail and hard hat. "Gotta go."

"Hey, come on," said Rudy. "This is the game of the year."

"Still and all, it's only a game," said Johnny.

"My son, the philosopher," Danilo grunted.

"What am I supposed to do?" said Frank. "Call in sick? For once, Johnny's right. It *is* just a game. It don't pay my bills if the Irish win."

"You're his foreman, Pop," said Rudy. "He could call in sick."

"Over my dead body," said Danilo.

Frank started toward the door, some fifty pounds heavier than in his high-school playing days but still moving like an athlete, on the balls of his feet, light and fluid.

"Frank?" said Rudy.

He turned around at the door. "Yeah?"

"Why don't you come to our touch game tomorrow at the lot? You haven't been around for a while."

Frank shook his head. "I don't do that anymore. It's for kids."

Johnny blew smoke in his direction. "When did you stop being a kid, Frank? I guess you've been keepin' the news to yourself."

Frank gave his brother the finger and left the house, slamming the door behind him.

"Enough talk," Danilo said. "We got a kickoff here."

"Let's hold 'em, Irish!" Rudy said, his enthusiasm suddenly a little forced.

Danilo shot a look at him, and he withdrew into his chair, concentrating on the TV screen.

4

After Sunday mass the following morning many of the churchgoers, still in their Sunday finest, the Ruettiger family among them, gathered at the CYO center and served themselves from a potluck table. They ate on paper plates at long tables that ran the length of the basketball court. The Ruettigers, including Sherry Wolinski and Frank's pretty but sullen wife of six months, Melinda, filled one table. Rudy had seen her smile maybe twice in all the time he'd known her. Father Zajak circulated among the tables conversing with the parishioners. He was a big hearty Irishman with flushed features who loved God, Notre Dame, good whiskey, and a funny story, in approximately that order.

Sherry pressed her leg hard against Rudy's under the table.

"What were you praying so hard for during mass?" she said.

"It's private," he answered. "And keep your voice down, will ya?"

"Telling your prayers isn't like giving away a birthday wish, Rudy. There's no jinx or anything."

"Who says?"

"I'm telling you. I read it somewhere."

"Well, some things you just got to keep to yourself. I'm learning that. You start broadcasting your business and it never gets done. Something bad's bound to happen."

"I'm going to be your wife. Nothing should be private from me."

"Yeah, I guess you're right. But I'm superstitious, Sherry. Sometimes I feel you can ruin things when you put them into words." He pressed his leg extra hard against hers and winked at her. "Don't think I'm trying to keep something from you because I'm not. Trust me."

Sherry reached for his hand and squeezed it. "Someday I'm going to understand you, honey. I swear I will."

Rudy leaned over and gave her a kiss on the cheek as Father Zajak walked up to the table.

"Danilo," he boomed in his husky bass voice, "it seems that your family increases in size from Sunday to Sunday. Is that possible?"

With a grunt, Danilo got to his feet and shook the priest's proffered hand.

"Betty and I are through having children—right, Mother?" he said, turning to her.

"I think Father Zajak is aware of that."

"But with girlfriends and wives," Danilo went on, "we are growing. Melinda here, Frank's wife, she's the newest Ruettiger. We hope there's plenty more to come."

Melinda nodded stiffly at Father Zajak in greeting.

"Well," said the priest, "the more Ruettigers, the better for St. Anthony's. You've always been a generous family. There should be many more like you."

Pounding the table for emphasis, Danilo said, "If any of my boys give less than ten percent of their salary, you just let me know, Father. Rudy is next—he starts at the mill this summer. And that gorgeous young lady sitting next to him, we're all looking forward to her joining the Ruettiger team one of these days."

Father Zajak stood next to Rudy and Sherry and put an arm around each of their shoulders. "Bless you both," he said. "You make a fine-looking couple, and I expect to see you here together on a regular basis."

Sherry glowed up at him and Rudy blushed, grinning at Frank and Johnny in embarrassment. As the priest walked away to greet another family, Rudy said, "Look, Frank—look who just came in. Tommy Bendel."

Frank shrugged and looked displeased. "So what? Big deal."

"Who's he?" said Melinda. "He looks dumb."

"Second-string defensive back for Notre Dame," said Rudy, and there was awe in his voice.

"Looks in great shape," said Danilo, lifting a huge forkful of mashed potatoes to his mouth.

"I can't believe he got a scholarship to Notre Dame," said Frank, and he made no attempt to disguise his bitterness. "I burned him twice when we played. There was nothin' I couldn't do better than him. A klutz.''

"Come on, Frank, he's good," said Rudy. "Not great maybe, but good."

"There's more to a scholarship than football, Frank," said Betty Ruettiger quietly, smiling sadly at her oldest son.

"Sure, Ma. Grades. You've told me that a thousand times."

"And it doesn't make it any less true," she said. "Notre Dame holds to high standards."

"I just don't get it," said Melinda, twirling her fork in her hand and scowling at it. "What's so fantastic about Notre Dame anyway? You all make a religion out of something that doesn't mean all that much."

No one said anything for a moment. Frank looked down at his plate, an uncomfortable expression tensing up his lips. Danilo cleared his throat, wiped his mouth with his napkin, and leaned forward against the table to address Melinda. "There's a whole history to this you should know about," he said.

"Now, Danilo," Betty put in. "I'm sure Melinda isn't the slightest bit—"

"Let me speak," he interrupted. He fixed his gaze on Melinda. "When I was a boy growing up in the old country, my father would talk about the greatness of America. He would tell me how immigrants with nothing could make a life for themselves—where poor Irish, Italian, and Polish boys could play football for a great Catholic university in the middle of the country. Our Lady—Notre Dame . . ." Danilo whispered the words with reverence. "These boys could go there and work hard and beat the rich boys from the great schools of the east—Yale and Army, Princeton and Harvard. And then when we came to America during the Depression, us Catholic immigrant groups, we were the objects of hate. We were scum. Lower than dirt, you know. And every Notre Dame victory on the field became a victory for us. Can you understand that?''

Rudy stared intently at his father. He had never heard him speak so eloquently and his eyes smarted with emotion. "Great, Pop," he said. "Tell us more."

Melinda looked almost angry as she said, "It's not the Depression anymore and poor Catholic boys can't even afford to go to Notre Dame now. It's one of the elite schools."

Danilo smiled at her, but there was no return smile. "But for me it's the same," he said. He tapped his chest. "In my heart, Notre Dame stands for something almost sacred. Nobody can take that away from me."

Frank glared at his wife. "I think you're a little out of line here," he said.

Melinda rolled her eyes. "I got a right to my opinion."

Rudy continued to stare at his father. "I'd like to hear more about your background, Pop. Stuff about the old country, about how you all felt."

"Enough talk now," said Danilo. "Let's eat."

But Rudy's mind was suddenly far away from the CYO center, from food, from family—even from Sherry, who gripped his hand under the table and held it against her warm thigh. He was recalling the words he had read in the brochure about Notre Dame that had been passed out to the class by Father Ted. Having read them once, then twice, he memorized them.

They scrolled across his mind now, and he savored them.

Notre Dame is a place for a young man to live in the pursuit of learning faith, common sense, peace of mind, solid citizenship, and future happiness. It is perhaps the biggest country club in the world, with lakes and golf and every sport. It is also a fine place to visit, especially on a football day when the championship of the nation is at stake. . . .

Rudy, caught up in the enchantment of those words, repeated the prayer he had mumbled under his breath in church that morning. "Please, Lord, find me worthy. Help me find a way to realize my dream. I know there's nothing all that special about me, except I do have this dream and I'll die trying to find a way to make it come true. Help me, is all I ask. And I promise that I'll try to do more to help myself. This is my prayer and I'll keep repeating it until I feel you hear me. . . ."

On the day of the trip to South Bend, students began to file onto a bus with NOTRE DAME in bold blue-and-gold letters stenciled on its front and on both its sides. Rudy lurked in the back of the line, seemingly not part of the group but merely an onlooker. When he was certain he wasn't being watched, he insinuated himself into the line, his head down, his neck hunched into his shoulders. Just as he was ready to step up onto the bus, Father Ted, who stood at the door checking off names on a paper attached to a clipboard, clutched his arm and pulled him out of the line.

"What are you doing here, Rudy?" Father Ted asked, his ever-present smile more questioning than usual.

Rudy studied his feet, stumbling for words.

"Well?" Father Ted's smile might be firmly in place, but his voice lacked its usual warmth.

"I'm going to South Bend," Rudy finally managed.

"Oh, I see. Do you have friends there?"

"No."

"Well, there's got to be some other reason then."

"When you read the announcement, I thought I'd go. I made up my mind to go. I mean it seemed like a good idea."

Father Ted shook his head and looked grave. "I'm sorry, Rudy. This bus is for students interested in attending the university. It's not a sight-seeing tour."

"Well, maybe someday I can go to school there. Maybe not right away, not right out of high school, but, you know, in a year or two? I can take special courses and all that. That's why I want to check out the place. Get a sense of what it's really like."

Father Ted clucked his tongue (Rudy knew from experience that when he clucked his tongue it was bad news) and now his smile was gone, replaced by a look of concern. "You don't have the grades for Joliet Community much less Notre Dame."

Rudy looked at the last student as he boarded the bus. "I know that," he said. "But can't I just go anyway? Isn't there room on the bus for one more?"

"I'm sorry, Rudy."

"What difference does it make? Who's gonna know?"

Father Ted rested an arm on Rudy's shoulder. "The

secret to happiness in this lifetime," he said, "is to be grateful for those gifts the good Lord has bestowed upon us. And those gifts are never doled out equally. We get more of one thing, less of another." He squeezed Rudy's shoulder as Rudy fought back tears—more of frustration and anger than sorrow. "Rudy," said the priest, "not everyone is meant to go to college."

With those words Father Ted climbed aboard the bus. Rudy watched as the doors closed with a pneumatic hiss and the bus pulled out of the school parking lot. He stood for a moment longer staring at nothing and then slowly started the long walk home.

PART

THREE

★

1972

5

A large iron door swung open and Rudy, wearing a hard hat and carrying a lunch pail, followed other mill workers into a dark, shrieking, steaming, cavernous hole. It was seven in the morning and he felt pulses banging painfully in his temples and a band of aching stretched taut across the back of his head. He'd been out chugalugging beer with Pete Sturges the night before. Now he was paying the price.

In the turbine control room, Danilo sat back in his chair with the grand manner of a king; his orders were carried out without question, and with no hesitation. At the moment he was frowning at a complex variety of gauges and dials. A group of workers with clipboards monitored the machines and waited for commands barked out gruffly by "the king," as he was called, though never in his presence. Those who worked under Danilo knew he was a fair man, but that

his temper was terrible to behold if he caught someone slacking off or disrespecting him in any way.

"Bradley," Danilo yelled over the din, "check the
feeder load on C-13 on the double. Duck—what've
we got on seven?"

"Forty-three and twenty," said Duck.

"Bring it down fifteen tight," said Danilo.

Rudy slouched into the room, yawning.

"You're five minutes late," Danilo snapped, glow-
ering at him. "Get your fanny down to B-Kettle and
check the intake valve. We got a cutout."

Rudy nodded obediently. "Sure, Pop." He turned
and left as Danilo, full of himself, in his element, continued to bark out orders. He gave off the vibrations
of a man who loved the role of king, even if his king-
dom happened to be a power plant.

Rudy made his way down a twisting catwalk,
through a maze of hissing boilers, vibrating pipes,
steaming turbines, and feeder belts carrying coal from
the outside. The noise was deafening and went like a
poison-tipped dagger directly for his headache and
jagged nerves. He stopped in front of a shaking boiler
and stared at it; it looked as though it would jump
right out of its bolts and chase Rudy down the catwalk. "Jesus," he mumbled. "Isn't this just great."
He picked up a rachet handle and started to turn it.
The steam started to increase in density.

"What the *hell* . . ." Suddenly Pete Sturges came
running down the catwalk, waving his arms wildly.
He pulled Rudy back and grabbed the ratchet handle,
cranking it in the opposite direction. The steam immediately narrowed down. Pete turned to Rudy, shaking his head in mock disgust. Shouting over the noise,

he said, "What the hell's wrong with you, Bozo? You pull tricks like this, you're gonna end up killing us all."

"Sorry," Rudy said, mouthing the word. "Hung over."

"What a weenie you turned out to be, Ruettiger. I had more brews than you last night and I feel great." Pete smiled his goofy grin, put his arm around Rudy, and walked him down the catwalk.

When the day-shift lunch break came at eleven, Rudy and Pete left the power plant and ate outside, under the shade of an old rusty water tower. Behind them, a series of coal feeder lines snaked up toward the giant redbrick edifice. It was marginally cooler where they sat and wolfed their food, although the temperature was well over one hundred degrees. Rudy used the edge of his dirt-smudged T-shirt to wipe the sweat from his face.

Pete finished his meat loaf sandwich and thermos of iced tea and lay back, his head propped on his lunch pail, munching on an apple. "What's today?" he said.

"Friday," Rudy answered. "Thank the good Lord."

"No. The date."

"August twenty-third," Rudy answered promptly.

Pete chuckled. "You never know the date. You hardly know what year it is. I wonder how you happen to know this particular date."

"Same reason you do, dummy. My birthday."

"Yeah, right. Hey, happy birthday, old buddy. Twenty-two big ones."

Rudy nodded as he peeled an orange. "It's starting

to go by too fast. And I'm not sure I'm movin' with the times.''

Reaching for a large paper sack he had brought along from his locker, Pete shoved it toward Rudy. ''Sorry I didn't have time to wrap it. Go ahead. Grab your loot before I change my mind.''

Rudy reached inside and pulled out a navy-blue jacket with NOTRE DAME stitched on the back in large gold letters. He stared at it for a moment, overcome with emotion. ''You bought this for me?''

''Yeah. In a weak moment.''

''Jesus, Pete, this is fantastic!''

''I guess that means you like it. I picked it up down at the surplus store in Niles.''

''They ain't cheap,'' said Rudy as he ran his fingers over the letters on the jacket. ''There's no way I'll ever be able to thank you for this.''

''Think of it like the Mafia,'' said Pete. ''You're in my debt now. I want to have a favor done, somebody rubbed out, I know who to call on.''

''Yeah, right.'' Rudy jumped to his feet and put on the jacket. ''What do you think?'' he asked.

Pete cocked his head to one side and squinted appraisingly. ''You were born to wear that jacket. It gives you that cocky mean jock look.''

''You think so?''

''I could've gotten a size bigger. You're fillin' out more.''

''Pumpin' iron every chance I get. Gotta stay in shape for you-know-what.''

Pete nodded. ''The dream.''

''I've put on twenty-five pounds in the last year,'' said Rudy. ''I'm one-seventy now. All muscle.''

"Between the ears," Pete said, grinning.

"You know the Irish start practice in a week," Rudy told him. "They have a chance to be national champs this year."

"I believe it," said Pete.

Rudy faked a pass with a make-believe football and jumped up and down. "Do you know Ara Parseghian is the first Notre Dame coach to encourage walk-ons? I read that in the *Tribune*. You know what that means, don't you? I got a chance."

Pete tossed his apple core in the general direction of a trash can. "You probably know more about that team than half the players," he said.

"Hell, *all* the players."

"And Parseghian, too," said Pete.

"I can't wait to get there," said Rudy. He took off his jacket, folded it carefully, and returned it to the paper sack. "I got a thousand dollars saved up. My do-it-all money. No—my dream money. That's better."

"You make Notre Dame sound like heaven," said Pete, "and you've never even been there."

"I know everything there is to know about it. It's the most beautiful campus in the world. *Life* has this great spread on Notre Dame. Did I ever show it to you?"

"Only about a dozen times."

Rudy punched his friend on the shoulder. "There's one thing about you, Sturges—one terrific thing. You're the only person who's ever taken my dreams serious."

"I have dreams, too," said Pete, "but smaller ones, I guess. Like a pay raise or having a boy with Rhonda the first time around. I'll never forget what my dad told me one time. I think it was when he was trying to get backing for this fast-food franchise. He was hoping to raise another two thousand, but for one reason or another it never worked out. He said to me, 'Pete, dreams are what make life tolerable. Without them life is an empty, lonely place.' I guess you're like my old man—a big-time dreamer. Guys like you need all the support you can get."

"Thanks for the jacket, man," said Rudy. He put his arm around his friend and they headed back to work.

Rudy's relationship with Sherry Wolinski had gone through some stormy periods since they'd graduated from high school four years earlier. Sherry had expected to marry and start a family, but Rudy had balked at the idea of settling down and working in the mill. He thought of the mill as a temporary thing in his life, not forever. One Saturday afternoon, on impulse, he and Pete went down to the navy recruiting office; they filled out various forms, and without telling either of their families, or Sherry, or Pete's new wife, Rhonda, they took the navy physical. If not quite a dream, the idea of a navy career had always been an option in Pete's mind, but he failed the physical; he had punctured an eardrum playing football at Joliet Catholic and was partially deaf in his right ear. Rudy, however, passed with flying colors. By the time he got around to telling Sherry and his family the news, he had received official orders to report to Great Lakes Naval Training Center for boot camp in three weeks.

Danilo was angry at first, but then slowly formed a

rationale that allowed him to accept the inevitable. At least his son was being a patriot; there was a war raging in Vietnam. At least he wasn't running away to join the hippies in San Francisco, reading love beads and smoking dope. At least he would be doing something useful to society. At least that's what Danilo told himself and told a very distraught Betty, who felt she was losing her youngest son forever.

It was different with Sherry. On the day he planned to tell her, she called him early in the morning, breathless with excitement.

"There's something you've just got to see," she said. "Are you dressed? Are you awake?"

"I'm awake."

"I'll pick you up in an hour."

"I've got some news for you," he said.

"Good news?"

"I think so."

"Well, tell me, hon."

"Later. It can wait."

Exactly an hour later—Sherry was always prompt and was intolerant of Rudy's chronic tardiness—she pulled up in her van. She gave the horn two short blasts—their signal.

When he piled in the passenger's side, she pecked him on the cheek and said, "Well? So what's the big mystery?"

"You first. I'm a gentleman, after all."

"Puhleeze. Spare me."

She drove off humming the Fifth Dimension's "Up, Up and Away," her favorite song. Five minutes later they turned into Calumet Street in a section of Joliet a step up from their own—more white collar than blue, even if slightly dingy around the edges. Sherry pulled up to the curb in front of a small blue frame house with a For Sale sign on a postage stamp of a lawn that was badly in need of reseeding.

"What's this?" said Rudy. "What are we doin' here?"

"Come on," said Sherry, jumping out of the van and running up to the front door. "Let's take a look around."

Rudy slowly opened the door but remained seated. He shook his head and found it hard to look into her eyes as she walked back to him from the house. "I don't want to, Sherry. This isn't for me. Not now anyway. The timing is all wrong."

She took his hand; she tugged at him. "I've waited a long time so we could start things off right, Mr. Ruettiger. I've been patient. I've worked at stupid shit jobs to save money for us instead of starting a family, like Emily and Joyce and a lot of my friends. They think I'm stupid to wait for you like this." She took his face between her two hands and pulled him close. In a sweet but deadly tone, she said, "You owe me, Rudy. I'm almost twenty-three. I've waited five years. Are you gonna make me wait forever or what?"

He allowed her to lead him into the house.

That night, on the telephone, Rudy told her he had enlisted in the navy. She burst into tears. Rudy wanted to say soothing things, but he had run out of persuasive arguments. Sherry seemed to have an almost physical need to have a family now, to settle down and have children and act the role of a grown-up; he wasn't nearly ready for the responsibility—ready for the end of things. Yes, that's suddenly what he saw: the end to his life before it had even begun. Stuck in the mill. Stuck with a lot of mouths to feed. Stuck in Joliet with no way out. Not knowing how to comfort her in any honest way—and after five years it was too late for lies—he remained silent.

"Rudy," she said, and he could hear the strain in her voice, "you know I can't wait. I'm sick and tired of waiting. You know that, don't you?"

"I know," he said.

"Don't you love me?" she said, her voice trembling and pleading at the same time.

"I love you," he answered. "But I can't base my life on that. There's all these things I have to do—that I have to find out—satisfy myself about. We've been over all this a thousand times."

There followed one of those long telephone silences between quarreling lovers that stretch the nerves taut.

"I love you," Sherry said finally. "But evidently that's just not enough for you."

"Don't make it any harder, Sherry. I know you can't see it my way, but please don't make it any harder for us."

"I won't be waiting when you get back," she said. "I'll return your school ring."

"I'd like to keep yours," he said.

"Do what you want to do. You always do anyway. I don't give a damn."

Sherry hung up without saying good-bye, something she had never done in all the years he'd known her, no matter how serious the quarrel. He sat for ten minutes staring at the telephone, wondering if he should call her back as he tried to isolate and under-

stand his feelings. He was shocked that he felt a
creeping sense of relief, as though a great burden had
suddenly been lifted from his shoulders. Then he
shrugged, let out a deep sigh, and left the room.

A week later, after making up, Rudy and Sherry
agreed to become engaged. The plan was to marry
once Rudy was given a permanent post in the navy.
Sherry was ecstatic and Rudy felt he had done the
right thing.

6

If there was a week that changed Rudy's life and helped to set it on an entirely different course, it was the one that followed. It was a week that would never fade in his memory, a week that he would think about—every day, if only for an instant—for the rest of his life.

When his shift ended on Monday, he joined Pete at Sloppy John's, proudly wearing his new Notre Dame jacket. Sloppy John's was a bar with battered wooden stools with no backs and sawdust on the floor, no women, and a lot of loud banter of the blue collar and sexual variety—a favorite place for mill workers to gather after work. Pete was well into his first bottle of Falstaff when Rudy, holding a newspaper clipping, rushed up to him.

"Look at this," he said, thrusting the paper at Pete. "Coach Parseghian's speaking at the Chicago Grid-iron Club tomorrow night."

"So?"

"I want you to go with me."

"Yeah, well, I don't know. Rhonda's been kinda touchy lately. She likes me home." Pete had recently married, and Rhonda Crotty, a plump girl with a jolly temperament, was five months pregnant.

"Come on, Pete, you gotta do this. I'm goin' away in two, three weeks. We gotta have some fun times before I go."

"Okay. That's a good argument. I think Rhonda will buy it."

"We'll be back no later than ten-thirty. Eleven at the latest. I guarantee it."

Frank entered the bar and, spotting Pete and Rudy, walked up to them without so much as a nod or smile of recognition. He grabbed the newspaper clipping from the bar counter and started reading.

"Ara Parseghian," he said with a sneer. "Jesus, bro, you just can't give it up, can you?"

"He's the greatest coach in the country."

"So what? You gonna get his autographed picture and kiss it every night before you go to bed?"

Rudy took a swallow of his beer and looked away from his brother.

"Hey," said Frank, "even better. Maybe he'll give you permission to wipe his ass."

"Leave him alone," Pete said.

"What did you say?" said Frank.

"Lay off him."

Both Pete and Rudy were now more muscular than Frank, but he still tried to play the role of the tough high-school football hero. He continued to bully them, and they let him out of habit, but the relationship had grown increasingly strained.

"Hell, Pete, as long as he talks this Notre Dame shit, he's gotta take anything comes his way. Maybe the navy will be good for him. Make him learn a little maturity. Face reality."

"You used to be a big Notre Dame fan," said Pete.

"Yeah, right. I used to collect baseball cards, too. I grew up."

Frank glared at Pete and Pete glared back at him. Rudy said, "Come on, you guys. Lighten up."

Pete waved a hand at Rudy impatiently. Although he rarely lost his temper—he was easygoing and laid-back by nature—Pete could be dangerous and unpredictable when aroused. Rudy had seen him in action.

"You know what Coach Gillespie used to say about you?" Pete said to Frank.

"Hey, let's knock it off now," said Rudy.

But Frank's eyes were fixed on Pete. He suddenly looked wary. "He said a lot of things."

"He said you had a lot of talent." Pete shoved up from his stool and stood inches from Frank. "But your problem was, you were too afraid of getting hurt on the field. You had no guts. That's the way Coach saw it."

"Go to hell, Pete."

"Coach used to tell me if you had one half of Rudy's heart and desire, you could've made All-Conference. Didn't he say that, Rudy?"

"Leave me out of this."

Frank pushed his chest against Pete's chest, shoving him hard against the counter.

"Coach said you were a pussy, Frank," said Pete. "All show. Nothing inside."

Frank grabbed Pete by his T-shirt, lifted him off the ground, and slammed him against the wall.

"What the *hell*," said Rudy as he charged between them and tackled Frank, wrestling him to the floor, where they started rolling around and punching each other. Pete and some other mill workers gathered around, attempting to break them up.

"Hey," yelled Danilo. He stood at the entrance to Sloppy John's, glaring down at his boys. He shook his head. "Don't nothing ever change?"

Frank and Rudy got to their feet, brushing sawdust from their clothes. They both looked away, shamed by their father's blazing glare.

"Sorry, Pa," said Frank.

"Get back to work," said Danilo. "You ain't supposed to be here anyway, boozing on your shift. You're developin' a bad habit there, Frank." To Rudy and Pete he barked, "You two take off. I want you outta my sight."

The next day dawned gray and muggy, and by late morning a steady drizzle had started to fall from a sky the color of pewter. Rudy and Pete walked outside the plant toward a maintenance shed, through billowing steam clouds rising from the great chimneys that mixed with the heavy, humid air.

"You didn't have to get into it with Frank," Rudy said. The scene at Sloppy John's the day before had been hanging there unspoken between them all morning. "I can take care of myself."

"I know you can. I guess it was something between

me and him. He's always treated me like a little kid, and those days are long gone.''

Rudy realized he still felt like a kid around Frank, and it bothered him. "Ever since he started working here, he's been pissed off at the world. The mill can do that to you.''

"Yeah, for sure," said Pete. "The whole thing is, he isn't a god here like he was in high school. He's gotta realize Joliet Catholic isn't the world.''

The moment they heard the shrieking siren they both ran to the shed wall and Pete picked up the telephone.

"Sturges," he said, and listened as Rudy watched him tensely. "Yeah . . . Yeah, right. We've had that problem before—rocker cradle halfway up. We'll handle it. No problem.'' He hung up the phone and turned to Rudy. "We got a jammed belt over at three.''

"Shit. Let's go.''

They approached the malfunctioning coal feeder belt and studied it. The line started at the coal piles on the ground and angled up three hundred feet to the top of the boiler system.

"Only one thing to do," said Pete. Holding a long iron wedge, he climbed up on the belt loaded with coal.

Rudy grabbed the sleeve of his shirt and tugged at him. "You sure this thing won't start up?''

"No way. Control room shut the system down.''

Nerves knifed through Rudy's gut, his bowels. "Let me go with you," he said.

"Stay here, okay? If this sucker does pop on, which it won't, pull that brake lever there with all you've got.''

Rudy nodded. "You got it, buddy."

Pete turned and carefully started to scale the three-foot-wide belt, holding on to the thin wire mesh on each side. To Rudy, craning his neck, watching him anxiously, Pete was like a spider crawling through a web.

Rudy's uneasiness increased as Pete reached the top of the belt. It just didn't look safe up there. One misstep, if one thing went wrong . . .

Squatting and pressing forward, Pete stuck the wedge under the belt and pushed down with all his strength, his biceps bulging. Rudy could see sweat gleaming on his arms. The belt strained, then released. Pete pulled the wedge out and held it up in the air triumphantly. "A piece of cake," he yelled down at Rudy. Rudy started to smile, but then his smile froze; his heart jumped in his chest, seemed to roll over. The belt had suddenly lurched into motion, knocking the feet out from under Pete. "Jesus!" he screamed.

Rudy watched in horror as Pete was swept up toward the coal crusher at the far end; he sprinted toward the brake lever and pulled—the *screech screech* sound the lever made was deafening, but it didn't slow the movement of the belt. Pete, grabbing desperately at the wire, was carried closer and closer to the coal crusher.

"You son of a *bitch*," Rudy screamed, falling on the brake with the full force of his body, willing the belt to stop. "Stop, please God . . . *stop*." There was a loud, wrenching groan and a crack like a pistol shot, and the belt finally stopped, but too late. Pete had disappeared into the crusher.

"This isn't happening," Rudy moaned to himself

as he leaped on the belt and ran slipping, falling, grasping up the incline. Reaching the top, he stopped and stared at Pete's mangled, lifeless body. He fell on his friend and tried to revive him with mouth-to-mouth resuscitation. But it was no good. Pete was gone. Rudy screamed into his radio for help. When another worker scrambled up the belt to help, he was hardly aware of him. Rudy stared down at Pete's face. His friend, dead. Only seconds ago he was alive, hopeful, young, just beginning, and now dead. The best friend he had ever had and would ever have, dead. Rudy stared at him, his eyes dry, his mind frozen numb, trying to take it in.

"No, no, no, no," he said over and over again. He let the worker lead him down, totally submissive, the way a child is after suffering a terrible embarrassment. "No, no, no," he sobbed, but there were no tears.

"Anno domini, deus te deum, de spiritus, de partum," intoned Father Zajak. *"Deo madre deo padre eternitatis . . . Amen."*

"Amen," the assembled mourners mumbled.

Rudy crossed himself automatically with his right hand and stared at Rhonda as she walked up and touched the coffin. She went to one knee and said a blessing, then stood. Father Zajak sprinkled holy water on the coffin. Sherry, weeping audibly, clutched Rudy's hand and squeezed until he could feel the hurt. His eyes followed Rhonda as she returned to her pew. She was beginning to show. She looked so young, he thought. With her baby face and rosy round cheeks, she could still pass for a high-school student. Rhonda was always laughing, always full of life, she and Pete

had known how to have fun together, but she wasn't
laughing now. Rudy looked away.

He tried to block it out, but the vision kept return-
ing. He saw Pete stick the wedge under the conveyor
belt and push down. He saw it again and again. The
image had haunted his dreams for the past three
nights. He kept hearing Pete's words: *Don't ever give
up your dream, Rudy.* Pete had told him that so many
times through the years. The world was full of dream
stealers and dream killers—people who had no hope
for anything better than what they had, and tried to
rob you of your own hope. But Pete had been different; he had believed in dreams, if not so much for
himself at least for his best friend, Rudy. I can't let
him down, Rudy thought. He's going to be watching
me now, watching every move I make.

Rudy went up to Rhonda as the mourners began to
leave the church and kissed her on the cheek. She
smelled of soap and he could taste salt on his lips—
her tears.

"You know he was my closest friend. Please let me
help in any way I can, Rhonda. Please . . ." His voice
failed him. He held her and wept into her dress, her
neck. "Oh God, I'm sorry. It's so awful. I'm so
sorry. . . ."

"It's all right, Rudy. It's all right. He's with God
now." She hugged him and ran a hand through his
hair. "I know how close you guys were. Thanks for
being here with me."

Rudy looked up and saw Frank staring at him intently. They hadn't spoken since their fight at Sloppy
John's. He kissed Rhonda again, asked Sherry to wait
for him a minute, and walked over to his brother.

"I'm sorry, bro," Frank said. "I know how you felt about each other. Since grade school."

"Kindergarten."

"It's hard to believe a thing like this when it happens. I mean you know it happened and your mind can't take it in."

"Frank—let's forget the fight, okay?"

"It's forgotten." Frank snapped his fingers and grinned.

"I'm leaving Joliet," Rudy said.

"I know. Great Lakes. Mr. Midshipman."

Rudy shook his head. "I'm gonna get out of it if I can. The navy's a mistake, like the mill's a mistake. I've got a dream, Frank."

"I know," said Frank. "You and Martin Luther King." His sarcasm—the habit of a lifetime—was hard to break.

Rudy disregarded it. "The navy's just a copout. Pete told me that in so many words. I'm going to South Bend. I've got to give this my best shot."

"What are you gonna do there? Get a job?"

"I have to see Notre Dame. I have to be on campus and see it. No more pictures, no more reading about it. I've got to be there."

"But what will you do?"

"I don't know. All I know is, I can't stay away any longer. Not after this."

On the walk home Rudy repeated to Sherry what he had told Frank. She listened in silence until he was finished and then said, "You shouldn't do anything rash right now. You're not yourself, Rudy."

"I think I am."

"Take a few weeks—as much time as you need. The mill can run without you."

"You haven't heard a word I've said. I'm not going back. I'll never set foot in the mill again. I'm going to South Bend."

"Rudy, this just isn't the time to try something crazy."

"Now *is* the time. I'm twenty-two. It's now or never, Sherry, and I'm gonna do it."

"We'll talk about it when we get home."

"We'll talk about it now. You've got to hear me, Sherry, you've just got to listen. I've run out of time. If I wait any longer, it will be too late."

Sherry pulled Rudy to a stop, turned, and faced him. "You can't make decisions like this on the day of your best friend's funeral. You're not thinking clear. You join the navy, then you unjoin it and decide to take off for South Bend, where there's nothing waiting for you. I mean you're just not thinking clear."

"I've never thought more clear in my life. You're gonna think this is crazy, but I'm doing this for Pete, too. He wanted me to go out and give it my best shot."

Sherry looked at him, tears streaming down her cheeks. "What about *our* dreams—a house of our own, a family, everything?"

"I have to do this alone," he said.

"Rudy—please. Wait a week at least. What difference does a few days make?"

Rudy blinked back tears. "I'm sorry."

She took a deep breath and pulled away from him. "This is it, isn't it?"

He nodded. "I can't help myself."

"One of us gets our dreams," she said. "The other doesn't."

"I'm not right for you, Sherry. Not now anyway. There's too much left undone in my life. I'd make us both miserable."

"Good-bye, Rudy," she said. "I guess there have been two funerals today."

He watched her walk away.

7

Rudy sat outside the bus station on a bench, a duffel bag between his legs. Even though it was a hot and muggy August afternoon, he wore his Notre Dame jacket. Danilo sat beside him, breathing heavily and cracking his knuckles nervously.

"I still say you're makin' a mistake, son. The mill's willing to give you a few weeks off. Without pay, mind you, but you gotta expect that."

"It's not the pay, Pop. I don't care about that. I just can't go back."

"And this navy business. I mean I just don't get that. How can you sign up and then waltz down there and say, 'Hey, I didn't mean it. See ya'?"

"I just told them the truth. I made a mistake signing up. My best friend died and I'm all screwed up right now. I talked to a psychologist, like it must have been two hours. I told him about my dreams and all, and he wrote a recommendation for my discharge. It's not even like a discharge anyway, I wasn't really in yet. I still might be drafted, I've got a number, and that's okay. If they take me, I'll go. I ain't goin' to Canada, Pop, with the hippies.''

Danilo shook his head. "I don't understand you. I thought Johnny was a screwball, but you take the prize. Here you've got a good job, a solid future at the mill, and you're throwin' it all away."

"Take a positive slant on things, Pop. I'm going for something I really want."

"You'll never make it," said Danilo. "That school's not for you and me. It's not for the likes of us. The sooner you get that through your head, the better."

"We'll see."

They sat in silence, and when Danilo began to speak, there was an unusual hesitancy in his manner, which made Rudy more nervous than he already was. He was used to the parental iron fist and could deal with it.

"I don't know if I ever told you this about your grandfather. He saved up all his life to bring the family to this country. He got a good job at the stockyard, a nice house in south Chicago. But when I was twelve, somebody sold him on the idea of moving to the country and becoming a dairy farmer." Danilo laughed humorlessly. "Imagine that—a *dairy* farmer. Can you just picture a Ruettiger doin' that?"

"It's not too easy."

"So anyway, he bought some land and about two hundred cows. Five months later all the cows were dead. They had some lousy disease cows get. It was the Depression and he couldn't sell the land or get work. One day he just up and left and never came back. My brothers and me, we had to split up, live with different friends and relatives.''

Rudy turned toward his father and stared at him. He had never seen Danilo cry, but there was a redness around his eyes now and his voice had a quaver to it that Rudy had never heard before.

"I don't think you've ever mentioned your father," he said.

"What I'm tryin' to tell you is, chasing stupid dreams can only cause you and everyone around you a whole lot of heartache. I know. I've lived through it. I don't mind telling you, it messed me up pretty bad.''

"My dream isn't stupid, Pop.''

"It's not just stupid, it's an idiot thing you're doing. Notre Dame is for rich kids, smart kids, great athletes, future leaders. You're a Ruettiger.''

"That's right. And I want to be proud I'm a Ruettiger.''

"Don't get me wrong. I'm proud of who I am. I'm a hard worker and a good provider. I've got a damn good life and you can, too, if you're smart. Frank will be taking over Plant Two in a couple of years and probably be making more money than me and Johnny. But Johnny's on his way up—he's involved in the planning for the new expansion.''

The South Bend bus pulled up to the curb. Rudy rose and hefted his duffel bag up to his shoulders. "You just don't understand, do you?" Although he wanted to leave on a peaceful note, he couldn't hide his anger. "I don't *want* to be Johnny or Frank. I don't *want* to work in the mill and piss my life away here in Joliet. *Listen* to me now while I'm still here to say this. I'm twenty-two years old—no kid, Pop, not anymore—and I've got my own life to live. Can you try and understand that?''

For once Danilo was silent; Rudy's passionate outburst stunned him. His youngest son had never raised his voice to him in anger before, and now he was shouting and Danilo had no idea how to react. *He* had always done the yelling, his sons the listening, and now the tables had turned and he was confused.

Rudy extended an arm as though to touch his father, then let it drop to his side. He walked to the bus and climbed on without a backward glance. Danilo stared at the bus as it pulled away. ''He didn't even say good-bye,'' Danilo muttered to himself as he sat there, his head bowed. He thought again of his own father, who had deserted him and his brothers, and suddenly he felt strangely young and uncertain. On the verge of tears. A boy once abandoned and now abandoned again, this time by his own son.

Rudy sat in the rear of the nearly deserted bus tensely staring out at the flat, midwestern countryside, but he saw very little. He didn't want to think about the strain of parting with Sherry. The strain of parting with his mother and father and Frank. He didn't want to dwell on the mill disaster and Pete's passing. As he so often did when life seemed to press in a little too close and the blues threatened to overwhelm him, he replayed in his mind the locker-room talk Knute Rockne had given his Irish team in 1928 in New York City just before they went out to play heavily favored Army. Notre Dame had a shortage of starters that year (Rudy had the history down pat), and besides, in those

days Army could still use players who had exhausted
their eligibility in college competition. The famous
1928 Rockne speech was on a record that Rudy carried in his duffel bag—but he really didn't need the
record anymore. He knew the speech by heart, word
for word. He was intimate with every enthusiastic
rise, every calculated pause and stutter, every dying
fall in Rockne's voice. Rudy could do an uncanny imitation of Rockne's delivery—the staccato speech, the
sudden rushes from thought to thought, the explosion
of emotion. Rudy could bite the words off and chew
on them, then spit them out, then lower his voice
quickly to a whisper, just like the immortal coach.
Strangely (and Rudy knew this, too, because he had
read all the Irish football lore and had retained it all),
1928 was the poorest season in Rockne's career:
5-4-0. Notre Dame had lost to Wisconsin and Georgia
Tech before they won the Army game, a game Rockne
felt he had to win to prevent a losing season. They
then went on to lose to Carnegie Tech and Southern
California. But in 1929 and 1930 they rebounded to
win national championships, and Rudy attributed that
success in large part to Rockne's stirring speech and
peerless leadership.

He looked up the aisle, making sure that no one was
within earshot, then began speaking in a low voice,
his eyes closed and focused on a locker room full of
players whose eyes in turn were fastened intensely on
him—Chevigny, Colrick, Niemiec, Elder, Collins,
Moon Mullins, Law, O'Brien, Brady. They all hung
on his every word. . . .

All right, Collins, Rudy began in his Rockne flat
midwestern twang, *you and Colrick play the ends.*

And the same backfield, Jimmy Brady at quarter-back, Collins, Chevigny, and Niemiec.

Now-w-w, it's the test of any team, men. Based on team play—the same as you've given all year—sac-rifice, unselfish sacrifice!

These are the fellows they say are pretty good, but I think we're better!

And I think if we get ourselves keyed up to a point, and when we're confident of that, why-y-y the results will take care of themselves.

All right now. On the kickoff—if we receive, the zone men will drop back to the receiver and block long—that old Notre Dame style.

If we kick off—which the rest of the teams want—let's run down fast—just as fast as you can run.

And then we go on defense.

And on defense—I want the center in and out of that line according to the situation. Use your old head!

And I want you guards charging through as far as you can go—on every play. Expect the play right over you every time.

And the tackles—I want you to go in a yard and a half and then check yourself. Spread your feet—squat down low—and be ready with your hands and elbows so you won't be sideswiped.

But I want the ends in there fast every play. Every play, but under control.

And you men in the backfield—I want you to ana-lyze it before you move. If you go for a forward pass, a zone pass, wait until you see the ball in the air—and then go get it!

And when we get it, boys, that's when we go on

offense. And that's when we go to 'em! And don't forget, we pick on that tackle that is weak.

We're going inside of 'em, we're going outside of 'em—and when we get them on the run once, we're going to keep 'em on the run.

And we're not *going to* pass *unless their secondary comes up too close.*

But don't forget, men—today is the day we're going to win.

They can't lick us—and that's how it goes. . . .

The first platoon, men—go in there and fight, fight, fight, fight, fight!

What do you say, men!

When the bus pulled into South Bend, the city of Rudy's dreams, he felt a sudden dip of disappointment. He opened the window and stared out at the houses, most of them small and nondescript and poorly maintained. How could such eyesores exist alongside his beloved university? The town looked a little cleaner than Joliet, but not any more cheerful. Then the bus turned into Joseph Avenue, and after so many years of waiting, of dreaming, of hoping and planning and praying, he had finally arrived at the Notre Dame campus. He caught a glimpse of the Administration Building's Golden Dome gleaming in burning majesty in the late-afternoon sun, and his heart beat fast with excitement.

He stepped off the bus and stared in awe at a large wooden sign with gold embossed letters—UNIVERSITY OF NOTRE DAME DULAC. Slinging his duffel bag onto his shoulder, he started to walk down an oak-lined lane. The picturesque campus revealed itself to him in its full splendor; the intense green of the wide lawns laced with undulating walkways, the slate-blue twin lakes, Mary and Joseph, dotted with students in sailboats moving among swans and ducks, the majestic dusty gold-brick buildings partly hidden by ivy and surrounded by the massed greenery of oak, maple, birch, sycamore, and pine, and the awe-inspiring grand Gothic cathedral of the Church of the Sacred Heart. He had to remind himself that he wasn't asleep and dreaming, that he was a part of it now. He, Rudy Ruettiger, was finally on the Notre Dame campus, strolling along on a warm August afternoon as though he had every right to be here. These trees, these buildings are now a part of me, he thought. I belong. Lighter than air, he walked across campus, a big grin on his face as he nodded to students passing by as if he were one of them.

He walked up Juniper Road and gazed, open-mouthed, transfixed, at Notre Dame stadium, a magnificent reddish-yellow-bricked bowl and the final mecca of his pilgrimage. Beyond the stadium, to the north, was the depiction of Jesus Christ the teacher that graced the entire south wall of the Memorial Library. Rudy stared up at Christ and thought, Touchdown Jesus. He knew all about Touchdown Jesus. When the Irish scored at the north end of the stadium, the spectators could see Christ over the goalpost looming in the distance—hence the name. All part of the history of Notre Dame, a history Rudy had studied with the care and concentration of a medieval scholar. And now that history surrounded him on all sides; he could see it and touch it.

A football practice was in progress on the field east

of the stadium. Rudy dropped his duffel bag on the ground, sat on it, and watched. A number of the players were familiar to him—especially the fullback, Andy Huff; Tom Clements, the quarterback; and the big defensive lineman, Greg Marx. He had rooted for them so many Saturday afternoons on TV, and now he sat on his duffel bag no more than a few yards away. He watched as Clements avoided a blitz with a neat sidestep and busted the defense wide open with a long pass downfield. Clements laughed and raised his fist in a pumping gesture.

When the practice broke up, Rudy continued to wander around the campus, inhaling the smells, the sights, the feel of this magical place he vowed would be his new home. He took the dirt path around St. Mary's Lake on the western edge of the campus and passed a small basketball court near the lake. It was in disrepair—the asphalt was cracked and warped and grass grew through the gaping spaces; there were no nets on the baskets and the rims were bent and rusted. A black teenager, fourteen or fifteen, was shooting hoops and going through a series of graceful fakes and fancy through-the-legs and behind-the-back dribbles. Rudy put down his duffel bag.

"Mind if I join you?" he said, and cleared his throat. He hadn't spoken in hours.

"Sure. Come on ahead."

"A little one-on-one?"

"Sure."

"My name's Rudy. Rudy Ruettiger."

"Garson Faulk. You a student here?"

"Not yet, but I hope to be."

They played until the sun was low in the west.

Rudy was drenched with sweat. Garson had trounced him pretty thoroughly, but then, Rudy told himself, basketball was not his game. Garson had a bottle of water and they sat on a bench by the lake and shared it.

"You in high school, Garson?"

"Yup. A junior."

"You get good grades?"

"Pretty good. B's and C's mostly. An A sometimes."

"You planning on attending college?"

"Nope. I'm gonna be a pilot. A commercial pilot."

"Wouldn't college be a help?"

"Don't help you fly better."

"I guess not. You live around here?"

"Out on U.S. Thirty-three. I bike over here 'cause none of the college kids use this old broken-down court. They got the athletic complex and all."

"You ever think of going to school here?"

Garson looked at Rudy, an eyebrow raised skeptically. "You must be shuckin' me. This place ain't for folks like me. If I went at all, I'd have to find me a vocational school."

"You sound just like my dad. He told me I'll never get in Notre Dame."

Garson continued to look skeptical. "So what do you think. Will you?"

"I'm gonna die tryin', I'll tell you that," said Rudy. He got up, picked up his duffel bag, and shook the young man's hand. "I enjoyed our game, Garson."

"It was okay." Garson nodded.

"See you around again, I hope."

"Sure."

As Garson mounted his bike Rudy said, "You come around here often?"

"In the summer, yeah. After work."

"What do you do?"

"Paint houses with my old man."

"Well, I'll see you."

"Sure."

"You know something, Garson?"

"What?"

"You're my first friend at South Bend."

Garson raised his eyebrow again—the intelligent skeptic who had already seen a lot in his short life— then slowly grinned and took off, doing a wheelie over a bump on the dirt path. Then he was gone, leaving dust in his wake.

Dusk had settled over the campus by the time Rudy reached the main building. He approached a white-haired guard.

"I need to talk to someone about getting in here," he said.

The guard eyed him suspiciously. "At this hour? The admissions office is closed."

"There must be someone I could see."

The guard continued to stare at Rudy. "Well, you could always talk to a priest. Maybe that's what you need, son." He pointed Rudy toward the Church of the Sacred Heart. Rudy entered the church, automatically waved the sign of the cross over his chest with his right hand, went up to the front, knelt, and said a prayer. A very simple prayer. "I love this place, Lord. Help me find a way to get in and be a part of it."

A priest entered, regarded Rudy as he prayed, then approached and placed an arm on his shoulder. He was a small man in his sixties with a quick smile and a bald head with fringes of white above his ears. Rudy, deep in prayer, turned around with a start at the priest's touch.

"I'm Father Cavanaugh. And you're . . . ?"

"Rudy. Rudy Ruettiger. The guard over at the main building told me I'd find you here."

Father Cavanaugh sat down, leaned back, and laced his hands behind his neck. Considering they were in a church, Rudy found the priest's posture curiously informal—more like bench sitting in a park on a sunny day—and it helped to put him at ease. "So what's the problem, Rudy? What puts so much seriousness on your face?"

"I just lost my best friend, Father. It was a steel-mill accident—I've been working in the mill for the last few years. In Joliet. I'm from Joliet. And after it happened, after the funeral and all, I just couldn't stay there anymore. My friend believed in me and I knew it was time I started believing in myself. So I got on a bus and came here. I have to make a new start."

Father Cavanaugh nodded, no longer smiling. "Have you taken the proper steps, investigated the process?"

"Yes, some. But I need to know more."

"Are you fully aware of the sacrifices you'll have to make?"

"Yes. I'm ready, Father. I'll do anything it takes."

The force of conviction in Rudy's voice caused Father Cavanaugh to look more closely at him, to search in his eyes for the truth of his words.

"It's very common for those suffering such a crisis

to seek an escape into the cloth. We usually recommend a grieving or cooling-off period first.''

"Escape into the cloth? I don't get what you mean."

"It's an expression we have to describe those fleeing emotional or psychological pain by choosing priesthood.''

Rudy stared at him, clearly confused. "You think I want to be a priest?"

Now it was Father Cavanaugh's turn to look confused. "You don't?"

"Nothing against being a priest, but I don't think it's for me." Rudy smiled for the first time.

"Why are you here then?"

"I guess I was rambling on and didn't make myself clear. I want to go to school here at Notre Dame. I've wanted it ever since I can remember. I've always watched Notre Dame football and dreamed of suiting up and being out there on the field, and . . . I don't know. It's like in my blood, if you know what I mean."

"Well, have you applied? You know that classes are starting now."

"No," Rudy answered. "My grades were never very good, even though I tried hard. Well, to be honest, I tried hard sometimes. But I was a kid then, I was immature. I've been out of school for four years now, I'm twenty-two, not a kid anymore. I'm ready now—ready to try really hard. To give it my best shot. I'll work twenty hours a day, if that's what it takes.''

"This university isn't for everybody."

"Anything. I'll do anything."

Father Cavanaugh studied Rudy carefully. "Tell

me, why is it so important for you to be part of Notre Dame?"

Rudy took a deep breath and said, "I guess I could write a whole book on that question. Like I told you, ever since I was a kid, I wanted to go to school here. And ever since I was a kid, everybody told me it couldn't be done. No way, Rudy. Not *you*. You just don't have the stuff. All my life people have told me what I could do and couldn't do. I've always listened and believed what they said—especially my father. He loved Notre Dame just like I do, but to him it was a God—something out of our reach, way above and beyond us. Well, I'm sick of people telling me what my limitations are. I don't want to let that happen anymore. Maybe what I mean is, I can't afford to. At twenty-two I just don't have the time to wait around for things to happen. I got to *make* them happen. I've got to get started before it's too late."

Father Cavanaugh rubbed his chin and seemed deep in thought. "Okay, Rudy, you make a compelling case for yourself. You're a very persuasive fellow, I'll give you that. But you know what they say—words are cheap and actions are everything. Are you just full of words? Be honest with me now. Are you here wasting my time and yours?"

Rudy shook his head. "No, Father. I mean everything I say."

"All right, here's my deal. Holy Cross Junior College is nearby. Just across the highway, in fact. I can only promise you one semester, but if you make the grades, I can guarantee a second semester. Then maybe, with a high enough GPA, you might have a chance of getting into Notre Dame."

Rudy broke into a big smile and stuck out his hand. "That's a deal I'll take," he said.

"I believe in fighters, Rudy. I hope you're a fighter."

"I won't let you down," said Rudy. "All I ask is the chance to show what I can do. I've been waiting for it all my life."

8

Early the next morning, having spent the night sleeping under the stars beside St. Mary's Lake, Rudy returned to the football stadium. It was still too early to report to Holy Cross, and besides, seeing the inside of the stadium was Rudy's first order of business. It was why he was here. If Notre Dame was Rudy's dream—getting a great education from one of the finest universities in the country, being the first Ruettiger to earn a college degree—the stadium itself was the heart and soul of that dream. One of the gates was open and unsupervised, and Rudy walked in and down to the field.

"Jesus," he breathed. "This is fantastic. . . ."

He dropped his duffel bag on the fifty-yard line and walked to the goalpost; he knelt down and felt the grass—cool and morning moist. "I'm here," he said out loud. "I'm really, honest-to-God here. I made it."

"Hey, kid," a voice yelled, breaking rudely into his

reverie. "This area's off-limits. What are you doin' here anyway?"

As if awakened from a dream and not totally oriented in time and place, Rudy looked up into the face of a heavyset black man in work clothes. His face was weathered and leathery, and his hair was gray at the temples; Rudy judged him to be in his fifties and sensed that he meant business.

He scrambled to his feet, and waving his arms to take in the entire field, he said, "This place is really something else. I've seen it a million times on TV, but the tube doesn't do it justice."

The man said nothing; he stared at Rudy stone-faced.

Unnerved, Rudy felt a need to fill the silence with words. He said, "One day I'm going to be running out of that tunnel onto this field. I'll wear the gold and blue. I'll be part of the team and the crowd will be roaring."

The man studied Rudy—looking down from his considerable height at Rudy's squat frame. He pointedly took in Rudy's duffel bag. In a lazy southern drawl he said, "Well, it's not going to be this day, mister."

"I'm here to play football for the Irish," said Rudy.

"Uh-huh. Does Coach Parseghian know about it? You informed him?"

"Not yet."

"Maybe you best tell him first."

"Yeah, you're right. That's what I should do." Rudy extended his hand. "Rudy Ruettiger," he said. "It's really great to meet you."

The man stared at Rudy's hand, then took it in his

own, much larger hand and gave it a surprisingly gentle shake. "Fortune," he said.

"Fortune," said Rudy. "I like it. It's a great name. Is it your first or last name?"

"Either," said Fortune. "Both. It's the only one I go by."

"Well, Fortune, I'm off to see Coach Parseghian."

Rudy picked up his duffel bag, gave Fortune a salute and a smile, and trotted off to the ACC, where Coach Parseghian's office was located.

Fortune, shaking his head, stared after Rudy.

The door was open to the outer office. Rudy walked up to the desk where a woman sat hunched over a typewriter pecking away furiously. He watched her for a moment, waiting to be acknowledged, then cleared his throat to help her along a little. She remained oblivious. He noticed a nameplate on her desk: FRAN MARTIN.

"Ah, Miss Martin," he said.

She looked up and placed a polite smile on her lips. "Yes? Can I help you?"

"I sure hope so. I'm Rudy Ruettiger. Please call me Rudy. I'm here to see Coach Parseghian."

The secretary's smile changed to a look of suspicion as she inventoried Rudy's rumpled clothes, his unshaven face, and his duffel bag that looked, as did its owner, increasingly the worse for wear. "Is he expecting you?"

"Well, to be honest, no. But I really need to talk to him, Fran. Do you mind if I call you Fran? I hate formality."

"Talk to him about what?" she said, her manner growing cooler by the second.

"Being a part of Notre Dame football," said Rudy.

"A what?" She studied his short, squat frame. "You?"

The door to Parseghian's inner office was open and Rudy saw him hang up the phone. "It'll only take a couple minutes, Fran," said Rudy, and he walked past Miss Martin's desk toward the coach's office. She jumped up to stop him, but Rudy was already in the door.

She followed, practically stepping on his heels, and said, "You can't just barge in here without an appointment. What on earth are you *do*ing?" Then to Coach Parseghian she said, "Coach, I'm very sorry about this. He just barged right in. I can call Security."

Parseghian, all the time staring at Rudy, held a hand up calmly. "It's all right, Fran. I'll take care of this." He leaned back in his chair; he appeared calm, but he drummed his fingers on his desktop. "How can I help you, son?"

Rudy moved around to the side of the coach's desk and, extending his hand, said, "I've wanted to meet you for years, Coach. Since I was a kid. You're a big hero of mine. I'm Rudy. Rudy Ruettiger."

After a momentary hesitation Parseghian took his hand for one quick shake, then let it go. "I'm pretty busy," he said. "What can I do for you?"

"I'd like to talk to you about playing football here at Notre Dame. That's why I'm here. I just arrived yesterday, from Joliet. I played high-school football at Joliet Catholic. I'm strong for my size and I love to tackle. Big guys, I don't care, it doesn't bother me. In fact I kind of like getting to the big guys. Well, I've got to admit the high-school days were four years ago.

I've been out of high school four years now, but that's a story I won't bore you with right now. My ambition is to play ball here."

Parseghian took in Rudy's crazed look and odd appearance, his wandering conversation. He quit drumming his fingers on the desktop and leaned forward. "Our walk-on tryout day was two weeks ago. We've filled all the spots."

"Oh, I'm not talking about this year," said Rudy. "Maybe next spring. That would work for me a little better."

"Are you a student here?" He cast an eye at Rudy's duffel bag.

With only the slightest hesitation, Rudy answered, "I'm at Holy Cross at the present time. But I'm going to be a student here. I just need to catch up on a few subjects and get my grades in better shape and then I plan to transfer." Rudy ran a hand across his forehead; it came away damp. Although the room was comfortably air-conditioned, he was sweating from a combination of nerves and too little sleep. "You see, I've been a Notre Dame fan since I can remember. I mean the passionate kind. I've kept statistics on the football team from 1960 until today. I'll bet I know stuff about the team's history even *you* don't know. I guess that's not a smart thing to say, but I'll bet it's true, Coach. I started at cornerback in high school. I wasn't the quickest guy on the field, and you can tell by looking at me I sure wasn't the biggest. But I led the team in tackles and my coach told me I was an inspiration because I worked harder than anybody else. I had the work ethic, he said, and I liked to kick ass—sorry, Coach, Miss Martin . . . Fran—but that's exactly how he put it. You heard of Coach Gillespie?"

"Gordon Gillespie? Of course," said Parseghian. He glanced at his watch. "I'm going to have to cut this short. I've got a freshmen workout in about five minutes."

"I've been working at a steel mill saving money and planning to come here," Rudy said, speaking faster now, realizing this might be his one and only chance to get his message across to the man who mattered. "My friend Pete, he believed in my dream of playing ball here and he told me not to waste any more time doing other things. He died in a terrible accident just last week. I was right there with him and saw him die. I just came from his funeral. It's Pete, I guess—Pete's passing—that's really concentrated my focus. I know what I have to do now—and I'll die trying, I can promise you that. If I ever get out on that field, Coach Parseghian—make that *when* I do, that's right, *when*—you're gonna see a guy willing to spill his guts and brains for the team."

Parseghian, who had grown increasingly concerned as Rudy's speech lurched around wildly, pushed himself up from his desk and walked over to the sweating and distraught young man.

Speaking gently, he said, "Son, I think you're in the wrong office."

"What do you mean?"

"You might be better off talking to Father Cavanaugh over at the rectory."

"Oh, I already have. He's the one who got me in Holy Cross."

Parseghian, steering Rudy to the door, looked at him, surprised. "He did?"

"Yeah. Wonderful man. He really knows how to listen. I guess that's what priests are good at. I told him everything I've told you and he promised to help me. He said if my grades are good enough—and they will be, believe me they will be—I'll be an official student here."

Coach Parseghian peered closely into Rudy's face. "Are you feeling okay?"

"Sure, yeah. I'm just great. I mean talking to you is like a tonic."

"You look pale."

"Well, I didn't sleep so good last night. A little nervous about getting started."

"When's the last time you had a meal?"

"Oh, ah, well, I guess breakfast."

"This morning?"

"Ah"—Rudy smiled sheepishly—"yesterday morning."

"You need any money?"

"Oh no, I'm fine. I told you I've been savin' up."

"Well, I'd get yourself something to eat, son. You've got big plans. You'd better keep your strength up."

Rudy studied Coach Parseghian's face. "I can tell you don't believe me," he said. "You think I'm just some nut wasting your time. But, Coach, I am who I say I am, and I'm gonna prove it to you." Rudy reached out and once again shook the startled coach's hand. "See you at practice one of these days." He gave Parseghian a jaunty salute, grabbed his duffel bag, and rushed out the door.

* * *

From the start, it was frustrating for Rudy to be attending classes right across the street from Notre Dame. So near and yet so far. He felt like a poor, starving kid with his face pressed against a window, watching the rich folks laughing and gorging at the banquet. He studied hard those first few weeks, but felt that he was in over his head and sinking fast. Four years was a long time, maybe too long, to be away from the discipline of study, and he was finding it difficult to concentrate. And besides his studies, there was much to distract him. Money, for one thing. He was worried about running out entirely; his thousand dollars was nearly gone. He had made a partial tuition payment to Holy Cross and his room rental in St. Joe's Hall was sixty dollars a month; he'd have to make other arrangements, even if it meant he had to sleep under the stars until the weather turned too cold. And when it turned too cold—what then?

At least he was beginning to make friends at Notre Dame. He was practicing for the Bengal bouts, a fund-raiser for Catholic missions in Asia and a long tradition at the university. The Bengal bouts, consisting of three three-minute rounds, were an outlet for amateur boxers—some athletes, most not. The boys loved to whale away at one another, and Rudy was no exception. His first Bengal bout took place the week after he arrived. He was matched—all five-feet-six of him—against a freshman defensive end, Jack Ritt, from Niles, Michigan, who was six-feet-two and weighed about fifty pounds more than Rudy and had muscles in his arms that stuck out like oranges. For Rudy, the fight was a test of his resolve. A test of his will to survive in this new environment. If he got through it on his feet—even better, if he beat this guy—he would begin to prove to others that you shouldn't judge by the outer package. You had to judge the heart, not the body, not simply what you saw at a glance.

Neither Rudy nor Jack Ritt understood the Queensberry rules or anything remotely resembling the niceties of boxing; they were in the ring to slug it out until one or the other of them dropped to the canvas. Halfway through the first round Rudy landed on the seat of his pants, stars swimming around in his head. He took the count of eight, got up, and charged headlong into his bigger opponent, fists flying, and slowly took the heart out of him. In the third round Jack Ritt toppled to the canvas like a huge tree felled in the forest. Through two black eyes and a bloody busted lip, Rudy grinned and raised his arms in triumph. He'd won his first Bengal bout, and when one of the onlookers yelled, "Atta boy, Rudy, you're a tiger, man," he felt as though he had truly begun to make his mark and find his true home.

But he hated the lie he was living. He couldn't bring himself to tell the guys he was meeting that he wasn't a Notre Dame student. He was vague when they asked him about his courses or where he lived, and when they went off to their dorms or classes, he would take the basketball he'd bought cheap from a kid at Holy Cross and wander over to the broken-down basketball court out beyond St. Mary's Lake and shoot hoops. One day Garson Faulk biked up and, without a word, joined him for a game of one-on-one. Rudy was more competitive than he'd been the first time they'd played; his boxing and his constant exercising were paying off. Although the kid could still shoot rings around him, this time he wasn't dead tired and totally winded when they finished.

When the game was over, Garson offered Rudy his bottle of water. Rudy drank greedily.

"So you got in school," Garson said.

"Not Notre Dame. Holy Cross. I'm hoping to transfer next year." Rudy looked at the boy. "You know something? You're the only one I've told the truth to. I've gotten to know all these people in the last two weeks, we have a beer or box or shoot pool, and they all assume I'm a Notre Dame student. Ain't that something? I can't seem to say, 'Hey, I'm a student at Holy Cross Junior College.' "

"You ashamed?"

Rudy thought about it. "Maybe I just want to be accepted so bad I let the whole thing slide."

Garson gave that some thought, then said, "I guess it ain't a big thing. Least as long as you don't fool yourself."

Rudy smiled and gave Garson a slap on the back. "You're still my first friend around here, you know," he said, and Garson looked at him with a shy grin.

Three weeks into his new semester, Rudy's first exams were looming and he knew he wasn't nearly prepared. The work was difficult and the hours of reading seemed endless. He forced himself to read over paragraphs three or four times, and even then he wasn't certain he had a grasp of the information. But he stayed up half the night studying, drinking cup after cup of black coffee to stay awake. Maybe when he actually faced the quizzes, a miracle would happen and the stubborn materials of science and math and English would suddenly light up clearly in his mind. But those fantasies offered him little comfort. He knew he was in big trouble.

When not worried about his studies or finances, though, Rudy was having the time of his life. He didn't even mind collecting garbage on campus—a job he'd talked his way into over three other candidates who had been interviewed before him—because it brought him into contact with more students. He was unfailingly cheerful and would introduce himself by saying, "Hi there, I'm Rudy Ruettiger. I'm a freshman, working my way through life." It was a line that usually got a laugh.

After classes one afternoon he approached the practice field. He knew it was off-limits, and at first he had accepted the rule, but more and more he felt as though he belonged. Because he loved the university and he loved the football team more than anybody else in the world, he reasoned, who had a better right to hang around and be a part of the action? In fact he was beginning actually to believe, deep down, that he *was* a Notre Dame student, and not only that, but a walk-on member of the team, or if not quite yet a walk-on member, certainly a future one.

A long fence covered with green plastic canvas hid the sight line but not the sounds of the Irish as they were being put through their paces. Rudy pleaded with a young, extremely officious student manager to let him inside to watch the practice. The stupid kid seemed to take pleasure in guarding the closed gate.

"Come on, man, give me a break," said Rudy.

"All practices are closed, fella. Nobody gets in without proper identification."

"But I know Coach Parseghian."

"Hey, congratulations. But that still doesn't get you in."

Suddenly there was a whistle, the collective roar of *"team!"* and the gates swung open. The players, dressed in their practice jerseys, came running through the gate, shouting and laughing and punching one another. Rudy, awestruck, stepped back. They're all so damn *big,* he thought. His bodybuilding and bench presses had improved his muscle mass, but nothing could add to his height. There was no getting around the fact that next to the smallest of these guys, he was clearly a shrimp.

He spotted Coach Parseghian walking toward him from the practice field, and as he tried to cross the tide of players to reach him, he was accidentally knocked to the ground by a big freshman guard nearly twice his size. Greg Warren, a defensive-back coach, reached down and helped Rudy to his feet.

"Thanks," said Rudy. "That was a pretty good body check he gave me. I'll get him next time."

Warren smiled. "Cocky, huh?"

"You got to be when you're my size." Rudy stuck out his hand. "I'm Rudy Ruettiger. I'll be playing for you next year." Greg Warren had a reputation for fairness and patience. It was important to Rudy that the coach remember him; every little bit of recognition counted.

The defensive coach ignored his hand. "I think

you're in the wrong place, boy," he said, and he wasn't smiling.

"Well, you see I'm here to have a word with . . ." But Rudy was talking to the wind, Coach Warren had already run to catch up with the players.

Parseghian was in a conversation with Joe Yonto, a grizzled defensive-line coach, when Rudy sidled up to them.

"Hey, Coach, how are you doing? Remember me? Rudy Ruettiger?"

Parseghian stared at him blankly. "Do I know you?"

"Yeah, sure. Don't you remember? I saw you in your office two, three weeks ago. I was wondering— do you think there's anything I can do to help the team?"

"Oh yes," said Parseghian, nodding. "Now I remember you. Look, I'm busy. I have no time for this. So if you'll excuse us." He turned back to Coach Yonto and they walked away from Rudy as they resumed their conversation.

Rudy spent that entire night sweating away at his books, and at dawn, needing some kind of physical activity to relieve the tension, he walked over to the football stadium and sat in the bleachers on the fifty-yard line watching Fortune, the grounds keeper and general handyman, hand-seed the field. When the older man spotted Rudy, he frowned, rose from his knees with a groan, and strolled over.

"Hey, boy, what'd I tell you about trespassing?"

"Listen, Fortune, I need your help."

"You ain't supposed to be here." He returned to his work and Rudy trailed along beside him.

"I want to be your assistant," he said.

"You want to be my what?"

"Assistant. I want to help you. I'm pretty handy. I can do more or less anything with my hands."

"Don't need no assistant," said Fortune. "See all those people out there?" He waved a hand at a number of workers on the field and in the stands.

"Yeah?"

"They work for me."

"But I'll work for free."

Fortune raised an eyebrow skeptically—he suddenly struck Rudy as a grown-up version of his friend Garson Faulk: smart, shrewd, and disbelieving.

"What's in it for you?" Fortune asked.

"I've volunteered a few times to do anything I can to help the football team," said Rudy. "Carry water, clean the locker rooms. Anything." He hesitated, embarrassed. "The thing is, I'm not a student here."

"You're not? What are you, like some kind of imposter?"

"No. I'm at Holy Cross."

"A hokey joker, right?"

"Yeah." He returned Fortune's slow grin. "Hokey joker" was the derisive nickname many of the Notre Dame students used to describe Holy Cross students. "But I'm gonna transfer as soon as I get my grades up. Anyway, I figured since I'll be playing football for the Irish next year, it would be a really good idea if I got to know the lay of the land, as they say."

Fortune's mouth hung slightly open; he looked truly perplexed. He stared down at Rudy from his considerable height. "Playing here? Football? *You?*"

"Yeah, I'm gonna make the team."

"You're nuts."

"Maybe. But I want to work for you. I'm begging you to give me a chance."

"You're also nuts to work for nothing. Nobody does that."

"I got another job where I'm getting paid," said Rudy. "Collecting garbage here on campus."

Fortune nodded. "Sanitary engineer."

"Right." Rudy beamed. "I like the sound of that—sanitary engineer." He took a handful of seed from Fortune and spread it around. "The thing people don't understand about me is, I'm not like other people. I wake up every morning singing when I realize I'm here, that I'll be here tomorrow. Next week, next year, and so on. I really love this place. I'm proud to be a part of the university"—he hesitated, shrugged, and grinned—"even though I'm not quite a part of it yet."

Fortune shook his head, turned, and went back to his seeding.

"Will you let me work for you?"

"We'll see," said Fortune. "Maybe I'm just nuts enough myself to let you."

9

A priest stood beside a chart in front of the classroom, lecturing on tectonic plates. He said, "The fissures created by glacial pressure and volcanic activity produce a deformation that creates our valleys and mountains and oceans. The faults and diastrophism shown here . . ." He poked at the chart with his pointer, and rambled on.

Rudy sat at a desk in the front row, in his Notre Dame jacket as always, taking notes intently. He sat in the front row in all of his classes, just as in high school he'd always sat in the back of the room, where it was much easier to dream the days away without being called on. He was determined to be a front-row kind of student now—alert, a hand raiser, ready with the answers. As the priest lectured on geological mysteries Rudy tried to write down every word he said; he was afraid of missing something that might be the vital link in the whole confusing process of understanding just what the priest was getting at, with all his charts and big words.

Sitting at a desk in the corner of the room was Rudy's new friend, a large, electric-haired boy named Dennis "D-Bob" McGowan. As he stared at Rudy, bent over his notebook, scribbling away furiously, he shook his head and grinned. When the bell sounded, Rudy kept his head buried in his notes, continuing to write. D-Bob got up, walked over to Rudy, and leaned over.

"What's with you, anyway, Rudy? You learning stenography or what?"

Rudy raised his eyes and gave his friend a don't-bug-me look, then returned his attention to his paper.

"Class is over, buddy. Father Lucas has gathered his papers, if not his wits, and left the room. You can quit pretending now."

"I'm taking notes."

"The question before us is, why? Everything he's mouthing is in the damn book, and the book says it clearer than he does. I'm only a lowly little teacher's assistant over here, trying to earn enough bucks to get through Notre Dame, and *I* know more geology than he does. And I don't know much, believe me."

"Come on, D-Bob," said Rudy. "I got to make an A here, all right?" He gathered up his stuff, stood, and walked past his friend to the door. He made his way down the crowded hall, D-Bob a few steps behind him. He stopped in front of a bulletin board and studied the notices for student housing. He frowned as he read the monthly fees; they were steeper than the sixty bucks he was paying at St. Joe's Hall. A pretty girl moved next to him and flashed a radiant smile. She was blond, slim, and dressed conservatively in the style of daughters of rich parents. In the tick of a second, Rudy was in love.

"Are you interested in a room to rent?" she asked. "I'm Dawn."

Dawn, with you I'd rent a rabbit hole.

"Hi, Dawn. I'm Rudy. Rudy Ruettiger. Next year you'll see me in the gold and blue."

"Fantastic," she said absently. "My brother has a house five blocks from campus. Only seventy-five a month for a room."

Only. Rudy tried not to wince in pain. "Well, I'm not sure, Dawn, but maybe. I'm looking at a few things."

Dawn smiled at Rudy (he noticed that D-Bob was watching them intently) and scribbled a telephone number on a sheet of notebook paper. She tore it off and handed it to him. "See you," she said, turned, and left, with a lovely movement of hips that Rudy couldn't help but notice.

D-Bob nudged him. "You don't have a clue, do you?"

"Clue about what? What are you talkin' about?" Rudy was still staring after Dawn.

"About how to get that A you seem so desperate for."

"Lay off, D-Bob." Rudy started to walk away. He liked his new friend a lot; he was fun to be with, plenty of laughs, but he was no Pete Sturges. Where Pete had been strong and quiet and kind, and always there to help you out when you needed it, D-Bob was brash and noisy and always into your business. He was also the brightest guy Rudy had ever hung around with. Rudy realized he couldn't be looking for Pete all over again; he'd probably had his one Pete for a lifetime; he knew you had to take friends as they came and enjoy them for what they were. But it was hard. Pete was still there all the time. But D-Bob was good for Rudy because he was easing him through his grieving process and also because some of that quick intelligence was bound to rub off on him. He hoped.

"I can help you," said D-Bob, nudging Rudy and winking. "Besides being an honor student at Notre Dame and a teacher's aide under the intellectually underwhelming Father Lucas, I'm available for extra tutoring. That's my beer money."

"I know that," said Rudy, turning to him. "So what are you telling me I don't know?"

D-Bob spread his arms and grinned. "I'm for hire, baby. Simple as that. Have brain, will travel."

Rudy shook his head. "Forget it, D-Bob. I can't even afford a room to rent."

His friend was silent for a moment and then said, "You need a hired head and I'm the best. Maybe we can work some other kind of deal. I believe in the barter system, in supplying services for other services. It gets around the crass financial thing. Money's the root of all evil anyway, which I don't have to tell you, being a Catholic. Church tells us that, right? So let's get beyond the ugliness of materialism—"

"What kind of deal?" Rudy cut in.

D-Bob stared at Dawn, who was talking and laughing with another girl down the hall. "You see that girl you were talking to?"

"Dawn?"

"Man, she is flat-out gorgeous."

"So? What kind of a deal? Come on, D-Bob, I got English comin' up. I can't afford to mess up."

D-Bob cleared his throat and whispered, "I've scoped out Notre Dame pretty good. You know, being the first coed year and all, everybody's excited, really up. The girls want to meet the boys. The boys display their plumage. The girls display their whatever—a regular prime-time mating ritual going on."

Rudy groaned. "Get to the point, D-Bob. *What* kind of deal do you have in mind? I've got exactly one minute before class starts."

"Well, here at Holy Cross I don't know too many girls, so I was thinking maybe . . . Well, maybe there would be a way. . . ." He shrugged and grinned, a touch of color in his cheeks.

"Maybe what?"

"You could introduce me to some fabulous chick."

"I don't know anybody around here, either."

"What about her?" He inclined his head in Dawn's direction.

"Dawn? Out of our league, pal. Forget it. Anyway, all she did was give me her brother's phone number. That's it. Tomorrow I'll see her in the hall, she won't recognize me."

D-Bob shrugged. "Well, so be it. Gotta run. Catch you later." He started to walk away.

"Hey," Rudy called after him, "maybe I do have a few leads. In fact, I do. I know a few girls—not well, but I know them. I know their names. I'd just have to talk to them a little. You know. Let me work on it."

D-Bob said, "Now you're talkin'. That's the spirit," and slung his arm around Rudy's shoulder. He whispered in his ear, "I wouldn't want this to get out, but as you can see, I'm desperate."

Rudy sat on his bed in St. Joe's Hall staring at his money. He had spilled all his coins and bills on the bed and had toted up the balance twice to make absolutely certain the news was as bad as he feared it was. It was. Thirty-nine dollars and sixty-six cents between him and oblivion. And not another salary check due from the university for his garbage-collecting services for six days. And his rent here at St. Joe's a week overdue. And twenty bucks he owed D-Bob, who didn't have any dollars to spare himself. And books he had to buy. A mouth he had to feed—but forget about food. He hadn't eaten a decent, full-course meal for the past three nights, and he couldn't see getting his teeth into one anytime soon.

He also needed D-Bob to tutor him; he knew he was slipping behind in all his courses, no matter how many hours he struggled with the books. Studying just didn't come easily to him. He had always blamed his poor grades on laziness, on not giving a damn, on having better, more interesting things to do, but he was beginning to sense that there was more behind his underachieving than that. All his life he had refused to slam his head against walls with no doors: it was as though there was no way inside where the knowledge was hidden, not for Rudy Ruettiger. Once in a while he would run around the room, frantically searching for an opening, but then he would become discouraged and give up. He realized that if he didn't get help—and soon—he was going to flunk out of Holy Cross. And that would be the end of his dream.

The end of Rudy Ruettiger.

So when he wasn't in class or in his room slugging away at the books, he tried to initiate conversations with girl candidates for D-Bob—not the ugliest and not the prettiest, but halfway decent-looking girls—desperately trying to drum up dates for him. But so far Rudy was batting zero in the procuring department. He was shy around these college girls. Most of them were so well-spoken, so well-bred. They were different from Joliet girls, different from Sherry Wolinski. You couldn't just walk up to them and get them howling with laughter over some corny joke, or give 'em a goose and say, "Checkin' your oil. You're down a quart." None of that business with Holy Cross or St. Mary's or Notre Dame girls. They had come for an education; they meant business, and D-Bob had monkey business in mind. But even so, Rudy tried to start conversations at every opportunity; he knew he was inept when it came to rapping with girls, and he put down his failure not to his beefy five-foot-six frame but to his crude operating technique. Once he got a little smoother, he assured himself, they would no longer rebuff him. And once he was on the football team, he dreamed on, then he would have his pick of all these incredible, heartbreaking beauties.

He finally did manage to get the phone number of a girl named Elsa Schmidt. By then Rudy was in a state of panic and had let his standard for acceptable physical attributes slip a few notches.

D-Bob took Elsa out for coffee and then met Rudy in the library, where they had planned to hold their first tutoring session. D-Bob slammed his books on the table, clearly in a rotten mood.

"Look, pal. I'm not *that* goddamn desperate," he announced.

"Sorry, D-Bob. I just haven't tapped all my resources yet."

D-Bob rolled his eyes in exasperation. "Well, try harder."

"Are you going to help me or not?" Rudy asked. "I mean I know I've screwed up so far, but I'm trying to line you up. And I really need the help. Otherwise it's back to the steel mill."

"Well," said D-Bob, "I guess it wouldn't be fair to base this deal on results only. You'll keep trying?"

"Damn right."

"Promise no more Elsas? We've got to have some goddamn standards here, okay?"

"You betcha," said Rudy.

"Okay, buddy, let's crack the books." He watched as Rudy eagerly opened his notebook. "By the way, tell me something. Why this insane obsession to get good grades. What's that all about anyway?"

"I've got to get into Notre Dame." Rudy hesitated, but then decided it was time to confide in his new friend. "I'm going to play football there."

D-Bob stared at Rudy, that incredulous stare that he was growing accustomed to. "You on drugs or something?"

"You know I'm not."

"Football?"

"That's right, D-Bob. That brown inflated oval pigskin thing you try to carry over the goal line. That's what I'm gonna do."

"I'm so glad I asked," D-Bob said sarcastically.

"I know you think I'm full of shit," said Rudy.

"But I want you to remember this moment. What day it is, where we're sitting, what we're wearing. When I'm out there on the field, I want you to remember this moment."

D-Bob pulled a pad of paper in front of them. "Okay, Gipper," he said. "Let's get to goddamn work."

10

An hour before dawn, wearing a sweatshirt and sweatpants, Rudy eased over the fence and onto the practice field. For the next hour he sweated his way through the exercise regimen of the Notre Dame football team: tire run, rollover, sled push (which, as strong as he was, he couldn't budge), wind sprints, and push-ups (one hundred with both hands, ten with the right hand, ten with the left). He had followed this routine every morning for the past three weeks, and his wind was improving, his muscle tone growing firmer. When he finished at the first sign of light, he walked over to the maintenance room and joined Fortune, who was accumulating tools for the day's work.

"Man, I'm beat," he said.

"You're crazy doing all that shit day after day," Fortune said gruffly, but grinning as he spoke. He was growing fond of Rudy; he had seen too many rich and spoiled kids come and go through his years working at the university. Many of them looked right through the black man as though he was just a piece of equipment—property owned by Notre Dame—but this kid was different. He was honest. A little crazy, maybe, but honest. He was genuinely friendly, and he was all on fire inside with this dream of his. Maybe he was even more than a little crazy, but Fortune would rather spend time with a nut than with the average "normal" kid who showed up at South Bend and believed the world owed him an education and a job just because he was who he was.

"How's school?" he asked.

"Well, you know I flunked all those quizzes last week. I was really down in the dumps, man, I mean far below sea level. When I went to see Father Cavanaugh, I was all ready to say, 'Thanks for the chance, but this ain't for me. I just can't cut it.'"

"Why didn't you?"

"I don't know. I guess I wasn't ready to give up yet. Then D-Bob said he was suspicious—I mean I crack the books till my head's bursting, but it seems like facts and concepts go through me like flour through a sieve. There one minute and gone the next."

Fortune nodded. "I know what you mean. School's no picnic."

"So he made me go to a language lab. They give these free tests. And you know what, Fortune? They found something wrong with me."

"Am I supposed to be surprised?" But Fortune said it in a friendly way and winked, and Rudy felt a degree more comfortable confiding in him.

"After all the tests, they said I got some kind of

dyslexia or something like that. It's like the words are all mixed up in your head when you read. They told me I've had it all my life and didn't know it."

"This dyslexia—is it a physical thing?"

"No. Just in my head. And they've given me a lot of exercises to get better."

Fortune nodded as he sorted through his tools.

"Hey, listen to me, man." Rudy grabbed Fortune's arm to get his undivided attention. "Maybe it's just a coincidence or something—it's only been a week—but I just got the first A on a test in my life. *The first*—ain't that something? I almost kissed D-Bob."

"Well, don't you get any ideas about kissin' me."

"Imagine—Rudy—me! An A . . ."

"That's great, kid. I'm really glad for you. Now grab those routers over there. We got work to do."

Rudy had been in the maintenance shed only once before, and now, as he gave it a casual glance, he saw a cot in the corner next to the shower.

"Hey," he said, "you live here?"

Fortune laughed, flashing a mouthful of silver and gold. "Believe it or not, I've got my own home. The mortgage is almost paid up. That cot's for when my sciatica acts up."

Suddenly showing keen interest, Rudy took in the room carefully. He stared at the windows.

"Come on, apprentice," said Fortune. "We got work to do."

They each lifted a heavy box of tools and left the shed. Then Rudy turned to Fortune and said, "Oh shit, I forgot one of the routers. I'll run back and get it."

"Meet you at the stadium," said Fortune, and kept

walking. But then he stopped and turned and watched Rudy run into the maintenance shed. Shielding his eyes from the sun, he continued to watch. He nodded his head when he saw the boy at the window. Reaching up. Unlatching it. Quickly, then, Fortune turned away and started walking. A moment later Rudy came running up to him carrying the router in one hand, the box of tools in the other. They walked down the tunnel toward the locker room in silence.

Casually, Fortune then said, "So, you in student housing?"

Rudy shot a glance at the grounds keeper out of the corner of his eye. "Yeah—well, not now. I was. I'm staying with a friend right now . . . in town."

"Ah, hmm," said Fortune. "Where in town?"

"Well, I'm staying . . . well—ah, shit, the truth is, Fortune, I've been sleeping in the garbage truck since Monday. I was at St. Joe's, but I couldn't keep up the payments. I still owe 'em forty for last month's rent."

"Pretty low on the funds, huh?"

"All my savings went for tuition. So—well, anyway, I can shower at the Holy Cross gym and—you know, I'm getting by just fine. No problem."

"Oh, hmm."

Rudy's excitement began to build as they turned a corner and came to a door, a sign over which read: NOTRE DAME LOCKER ROOM. This was the moment he had been looking forward to for years. Went to sleep thinking about. Dreamed about. As Fortune inserted a key in the lock Rudy had to restrain himself from jumping up and down like a kid.

"So this is it," he said.

"Yup," said Fortune. "Where it all starts and fin-ishes." He pushed open the door.

Rudy walked inside slowly, his mouth wide open, his heart thumping with excitement. He had read that the team had been using this same space since 1930, since the Rockne glory years. His eye caught a bronze plaque with an engraved inscription. He moved closer, carefully running his fingers over the plaque and mumbled the inscription aloud:

"I've got to go, Rock, it's all right. I'm not afraid. Sometime when the team is up against it, when things are going wrong and the breaks are beating the boys, tell them to go in there with all they've got and win just one for the Gipper. I don't know where I'll be then, Rock, but I'll know about it and I'll be happy. . . ."

Rudy backed away a step, feeling moisture gather in his eyes. "Wow," he whispered. He looked over at Fortune, who was busy arranging his tools on the floor. After staring at the plaque for another long awe-struck moment, Rudy wandered around the locker room chanting names as if part of an incantation.

"Knute Rockne," he said. "Frank Leahy. Moose Krause. Angelo Bertelli. Johnny Lujack. Leon Hart. Terry Hanratty. John Huarte. Jim Seymour. Jack Snow . . ." He moved to one of the lockers and touched it. Looking over at Fortune, he said, "Paul Hornung could've dressed here. Imagine that—isn't that something?"

Ignoring Rudy, Fortune examined a torn seam in the rug.

"Where did Nick Eddy have his locker? I wonder," Rudy said. "Man, I loved that guy. What a fantastic runner."

"Time for work. No more goofin' off now."

"Yeah, right." Rudy grabbed a stool, placed it in the center of the room, and stood on it. Doing his Rockne imitation, he yelled out, " 'We're going inside of 'em, we're going outside of 'em—and when we get them on the run once, we're going to keep 'em on the run. What do you say, men!' "

Fortune stared up at Rudy, trying to put on his strict, no-nonsense face, but in spite of himself he smiled.

Around midnight Rudy approached the maintenance shed, peering around nervously to make certain he was unobserved. He reached up and tested the window; it gave easily at his touch and he climbed in. He took off his sweater and covered the lamp so that the light wouldn't be too obvious when he turned on the switch. He noticed a paper sack on the table that hadn't been there earlier in the day. He opened it and pulled out two cartons, both still warm to the touch— one contained rice and the other Chinese snow peas and beef. The smell made his mouth water.

In the corner of the room was a bundle—two blankets and a sheet. Rudy was positive they hadn't been there earlier, either. He shook his head and a slow grin broke like daylight across his features. "Fortune, you're somethin' else. I love you, man. I love you." He wrapped one of the blankets around his shoulders like a poncho (the nights were growing cold) and attacked the food with all the gusto of a healthy but starving twenty-two-year-old.

Fall was turning the trees of Notre Dame a brilliance of yellow and red and brown and pink and gold. As Rudy walked toward the library to meet D-Bob, he thought the campus looked even more beautiful at this moment, if possible, than when he'd first laid eyes on it. He inhaled the crisp autumn air and felt like singing with joy.

At that moment D-Bob came running up to him.

"Hey, D-Bob," he said, greeting his friend with a hand slap.

"Rudy. Hey, Gipper, my man. Too nice a day for the library, right? Let's motor around, take in the sights, make some girl happy. By the way, I got a little something for you." He pulled out a laminated card and held it in front of Rudy, waving it back and forth. "You are now the proud possessor of a Notre Dame gym pass, which means you join the ranks of the privileged young of this Michiana area we presently call home. The place crawls with all the big jocks. In other words, you are now a pig in shit."

"You did it!" said Rudy. "You're a genius."

"A given," said D-Bob. He cleared his throat. "I presume you recall our deal."

"I do your laundry for two months. Yeah."

"The fact is, this was a little harder to pull off than anticipated," said D-Bob. "I'm afraid the laundry's only part of it. You'll have to set me up with girls for an entire semester."

"A semester? Jesus, D-Bob."

D-Bob shrugged and started to return the card to his wallet.

"Okay," said Rudy, grabbing for the card. "I'll do what I can."

"Maybe you should start right now," said D-Bob, pointing. "There's your mission."

Rudy turned and saw a pretty, curly-haired brunette—pretty on the verge of beautiful—sitting behind a folding table with a sign propped up beside it: STUDENT ACTIVITIES. He shook his head emphatically. "Impossible. Forget it. That's Mary McDonough."

"So? Who's Mary McDonough? What makes her so special?"

"She only happens to be about the most popular freshman on campus, is all. Plus her dad is some kind of rich automotive executive from Michigan. Grosse Pointe or someplace. Plus she's beautiful."

"That she is. That she definitely is."

"Plus I think she's dating some important jock."

"Nonetheless and notwithstanding, it's your job to give it a shot. Your very *best* shot."

"Out of our league," said Rudy, "by light-years."

"Don't ever sell yourself short, Gipper. And more to the point, don't ever sell *me* short."

"D-Bob, I'm telling you. This has failure written all over it."

"Tell her I'm a Field, a Marshall Field. Use your charm, your friendliness, your wonderful open disposition. Like, whatever. Now go."

Rudy drew in a deep breath and slowly walked up to Mary McDonough. He couldn't tell D-Bob, it was too embarrassing, but in recent weeks he had developed his own fixation on Mary. She always seemed to be in the middle of a crowd of friends, laughing and looking spectacular—flashing white teeth, large dark eyes, beautiful silky dark hair, and rosy cheeks—and lately Rudy had taken to thinking about her when she wasn't around. A bad sign. He had school to think about, not girls—and especially not girls like Mary, who wouldn't give guys like him the time of day.

He stood in front of her table, cleared his throat, opened his mouth to speak, but no words came out. She looked up and smiled into his eyes. Her smile was a pure ten and turned his limbs to mush.

"Are you interested in joining a student activity?" she asked. Her voice, soft and low, went with the rest of her.

"Oh yes, absolutely." *Absolutely?* Where did *that* word come from? he wondered. It wasn't part of his vocabulary and he definitely wasn't himself. The only student activity he could think of at the moment was necking with Mary McDonough in a dark room.

She handed him a sheet of paper. "Here are your choices," she said.

Rudy studied the sheet, or pretended to, all the time feeling her eyes on him. Burning him all over. Couldn't it be like this forever? Mary's eyes on him, just the two of them together out of all the people in the world?

"Is there anything on the sheet that interests you?" she asked.

"Oh yeah. Everything."

"You're only allowed two choices."

Rudy, hearing a loud throat clearing from D-Bob, leaned across the table. "See that guy over there?" he said, motioning with a movement of his head toward D-Bob.

Mary glanced over at D-Bob, frowning slightly and instinctively pulling back from Rudy. "Yes. What about him?"

"Well, he's a . . . he's . . . I don't know how to say it."

"Yes?" she said.

"Well, he's a jerk. Well, not a jerk exactly, but he's kind of *slow*. So if you could give him a wave, to just kind of humor him?"

Mary squinted (oh God, her eyes were so large and dark and incredibly sexy!) at Rudy as though *he* was slow. Then, pursing her lips in a small, embarrassed smile, she waved casually in the general direction of D-Bob. With a big, foolish grin, D-Bob waved back enthusiastically.

"Thanks," said Rudy.

Mary pointed to her sign-up sheet. All business. "Well?"

After quickly scanning the list of activities, Rudy said, "Ah, choir. I sang in choir in high school, and— wait a minute. What's this? Football Boosters? What is this?"

"We organize pep rallies," said Mary. "We paint the helmets the night before the game."

"That's me," said Rudy, his voice rising with excitement. "Definitely me. Where do I sign?"

Mary smiled at his enthusiasm, then said, "Are you a Notre Dame student?"

This was one of Rudy's worst moments—the kind he feared the most. Mary McDonough was not someone he enjoyed lying to, but what choice did he have?

In his mind he already *was* a Notre Dame student; the truth was simply too painful and embarrassing to reveal to such a beautiful girl. "Of course," he said after only the slightest pause. "How can you even ask? Don't I look like one?"

"We're supposed to check everybody out."

"Well, I'm Notre Dame blue and gold through and through."

Rudy grinned and Mary returned his smile. "Me, too," she said. "I'm really excited at being in the first class of women students. We're making history."

"You sure are," said Rudy, his grin growing wider. "And it's the best thing that could possibly happen to this place." He leaned forward and signed his name.

"First meeting for the Boosters is tomorrow night at the ACC," Mary told him.

"You're part of it, right?" he asked.

"Freshman cochair."

"Great. That's really great."

Rudy stood for a moment smiling at the unresponsive Mary. There was someone behind him waiting to speak to her and she was politely waiting for Rudy to move on.

"Well, I'll see you then," he said.

"Sure," she said vaguely, already beaming a welcoming smile at the next person in line. It was just as warm a smile, Rudy realized sadly, as the one she'd given him. She obviously had that smile down pat, and it was about as personal as someone shaking your hand in a receiving line.

He turned awkwardly away from her and walked back to the eagerly waiting D-Bob.

"Well?" he said. "A homer?"

Rudy shook his head.

"Come on, man, at least a single? A little scratch single?"

"Strikeout, D-Bob. Didn't get my bat on the ball."

Rudy began walking, his head down, his hands deep in his pockets. D-Bob followed along beside him. "Christ, you looked like you were in. All that chatting and smiling at each other. I was getting hot just watching the two of you."

"She has a boyfriend," said Rudy. "Football player. Quarterback."

D-Bob looked hard at Rudy. "Yeah?"

"Yeah."

"If that's the case, what's the big shit-eating smile all about? You look awfully goddamn happy about it."

Off in his own world—a world in which he existed solely for Mary McDonough and she for him, where the course of true love ran smoothly and all endings were happy ones—Rudy tuned D-Bob out.

11

He entered the athletic complex clutching the false ID that D-Bob had managed to finagle for him in return for a semester's worth of dates or introductions to acceptably good-looking girls, plus doing his laundry. He casually tossed his card to a squinty-eyed student manager, who nudged his glasses up the bridge of his nose and examined it closely.

"David Constantino," mumbled the student manager. He peered up at Rudy, wrinkling his face into a prune. "You don't resemble this photograph."

"I've gained a lot of weight," said Rudy. "Last year, when this picture was taken, I had mono."

"Really?" said the student manager, showing sudden interest, his expression brightening. "I had mono last year myself. A real bitch, right?"

"A real bitch," Rudy agreed.

"Screws up your liver, your spleen, and I don't know what all. I had no appetite for *weeks*."

"Me neither."

" 'The kissing disease,' it's called. But I actually don't know how I contracted it. I wasn't kissing anybody."

Rudy nodded.

"Are you completely over it now?" asked the student manager.

"Yeah, I'm okay now."

At that moment three Notre Dame football players sauntered up (and walked right in without showing their passes, Rudy noticed). He recognized them—Jamie O'Hare, blond and handsome, a freshman halfback with a bright future; Steve Mateus, a lineman with huge, clublike arms; and Roland Steele, a small catlike cornerback with a wide grin and a huge Afro. Rudy had seen them in practice for weeks and felt as though they were already close buddies of his, even though they didn't know him from Adam.

"They're freshmen," said the student manager, watching Rudy watching them. "The guy in front, Jamie O'Hare, he was the most heavily recruited high-school halfback in the country."

"I know who he is," said Rudy, trying to hide his impatience. "I've been watching him practice."

"If you ask me, though, O'Hare needs to get cold-cocked a few times. Bring him down to earth with the rest of us lesser mortals. Frankly, he acts like he's just too grand for this world." He handed Rudy his card. "Have fun. See you around."

"Yeah, thanks," said Rudy.

He changed and entered the weight room, where the football players were working out. Steve Mateus was grunting and screaming as he pressed two hundred forty pounds of weight. Roland Steele was doing chin-ups at an impressively fast clip. He counted as he did them—"Fifty-two, fifty-three, fifty-four . . ." And Jamie O'Hare was curling barbells. Rudy stood near them, following their movements closely, wanting to be accepted by them. This was the only fraternity that mattered—the fraternity of Notre Dame football players. For Rudy, all the money and power in the world could never compare with this.

"Hey, how you doing?" he said to O'Hare.

The player acted as though he wasn't there. Finally, Rudy couldn't stand being shunned, treated like somebody invisible, like a member of the insect world. He approached O'Hare and said, "Hi, I'm Rudy. Rudy Ruettiger. I played ball in Joliet. For Joliet Catholic."

The golden-haired halfback ignored him.

"Hey, Jamie, I know a terrific exercise for quadriceps. Let me show it to you. It might help your first step."

O'Hare looked Rudy up and down and wrinkled his nose as though he was smelling something rotten. "Who the hell asked you?"

Raising his hands, palms out, in a gesture of peace, Rudy said, "Look, I'm sorry if I said the wrong thing. I was just trying to help is all."

"You think I never been in a weight room before?"

"Hey, Jamie, we might as well be friends," said Rudy. "I'm going to be your teammate next year."

Jamie O'Hare's laugh was loud and uninfectious. "In your dreams, shrimp," he said. "In your dreams." He turned to his friends. "Who let *this* guy in?"

Steve Mateus walked up to O'Hare and gave him a

shove. "Come on, Prince. We're doing the circuit in fifteen clicks."

O'Hare rolled his eyes at Mateus as he tilted his head in Rudy's direction. "This character is hassling me, man."

Mateus turned slowly toward Rudy and leveled his two-hundred-sixty-pound lineman's glower at him. He pointed a thick finger and poked it against Rudy's chest. "Leave my buddy alone. Get it, ass-wipe? He's the franchise and you're a piece of shit. Simple as that. Want me to draw you a diagram?"

Rudy's eyes widened and he took a step backward. It wasn't physical fear that made him retreat—he was not afraid of pain and he even welcomed combat—but some level of unfocused anger in the lineman's character that he found hard to accept.

Roland Steele, having completed his chin-ups, dropped from the bar and yelled out to Mateus, who was twice his size, "Come on, Steve, cool it. Leave the kid alone. He didn't do nothing."

"He's buggin' the Prince."

"Forget it, Steve," said O'Hare. "He must be one of my many admirers." He gave Mateus an exaggerated wink.

Mateus shrugged and moved on to the next exercise. Rudy started to thank Steele for coming to his defense, but Steele had already dropped to the floor to start a series of push-ups.

The Football Boosters, working as an assembly line, were hard at work in the equipment room removing the face gear from football helmets, scrubbing them down, putting on masking tape, spraying the helmets with a brilliant gold paint, laying the helmets on a dryer board, and finally buffing and polishing their surfaces to a high sheen. This activity was carried on with a lot of joking and laughter, and Rudy was thrilled to be a part of it—doing something for the football team and making new friends at the same time. And—certainly far from least—being in close proximity to Mary McDonough. He completed work on a helmet, and seeing that for the moment she was alone, he walked over to her.

"Isn't this fantastic, Mary?" he said. "Did you know they put real twenty-four-karat gold in the paint?"

She looked at him, puzzled, trying to place him. "What's your name again?"

"Rudy. Rudy Ruettiger? Don't you remember me? We had a nice, long talk the other day when I signed up for the Boosters."

"I meet a lot of students in my job," she said. "You do look familiar."

"Well, at least I look familiar," he said, grinning.

She didn't return his smile. "I need your student ID to get your card section pass," she said.

"Oh, wouldn't you know it? I don't have it on me. I left it in the dorm. But I'll have it later . . . tomorrow."

"I'm supposed to turn in the names tonight," she said.

He forced an extra bright smile from the side of his mouth—his debonair, devil-may-care smile that always used to wow Sherry Wolinski. It seemed, though, to have decidedly less of an effect on Mary

McDonough. "Come on, Mary," he said. "Can't you let it slide, just this once?"

Her eyes darting around, checking out the activity in the room, she said, "Sorry. You bring your ID and you can work the next game."

"Okay," he said, and he looked so crestfallen that Mary—who felt quick compassion for others—reached out and touched him. "You coming to Corby's? It's where we all go after we're through here."

Like a dog who had been scolded and then petted, Rudy was suddenly tail-waggingly happy. He said, "Oh thanks. Sure, I'll be there."

A popular Notre Dame hangout, Corby's was packed to the rafters. Rudy, holding two beers aloft, swiveled and dodged his way through the crowd until he reached Mary and her group. As always, she seemed to be a magnet, drawing others to her. The happy center of attention, Rudy thought. And why not? He offered her one of the beers.

She shook her head. "I'm not twenty-one," she said.

"Oh, I'm sorry."

She stared at Rudy holding the beers—other eyes were on him, too—and he realized an explanation was in order.

"I'm twenty-two," he said with a shrug and a grin. "What happened was, I took some time off after high school—traveling, working. You know, the usual. But I'd always planned to return for college after I'd grown up a little and seen something of the world. And here"—he spread his arms—"I am." He directed this speech to Mary exclusively, trying to gauge her reaction. He knew it might be nothing more than his overactive imagination, but he thought he saw a spark of interest in her eyes; she seemed to look at him as though she were seeing him for the first time—not as a student in the job, part of the campus scenery, but as . . . *Rudy Ruettiger.*

"It's awfully hot in here, Mary," he said. "Maybe we could go down the street to Malone's Pub. I'll buy you dinner."

With what? he thought. Do I have enough dough?

He saw that he had lost her; something in her eyes flattened out. "I don't think so."

But he couldn't let go. If only he could light that spark of interest in her eyes again . . . "What's your major?" he said.

"Journalism." She was looking around the room now, clearly bored. He was a piece of furniture to her. Then her eyes lighted up; her shoulders straightened and she came alive. She smiled at someone over Rudy's shoulder. He turned to see Jamie "The Prince" O'Hare striding toward them, bouncing on his toes, swinging his shoulders—the picture, Rudy admitted sadly, of the classic top jock.

He rose from the bar stool and held out his hand. "Hey, Jamie," he said, "how's it goin'?"

O'Hare stopped and stared at Rudy. "Do I know you?"

Rudy nodded. "The weight room?"

A faint look of distaste crossed O'Hare's face. "Oh yeah," he said. "Now I remember you." But then his glance reached out for Mary McDonough like a hot and eager hand, moving all over her. His smile was white and dazzling. "I don't think I've had the pleasure," he said with a slight bow.

"You smiled at me when you came in like you knew me," Mary said.

"And you smiled back," said O'Hare. "And here I am."

Rudy was eager to impress them both and to be a part of them in some small way. He said, "Jamie, I want you to meet a good friend of mine, Mary Mc-Donough. Mary—Jamie O'Hare."

Mary's and O'Hare's eyes locked, leaving them in one space with Rudy on the outside. But for the sake of politeness Mary turned to Rudy and said, "How do you two know each other?"

"The weight room, like I said. We were working out together."

O'Hare's eyes narrowed. "I work out every day with Mateus and Steele."

Rudy explained quickly to Mary, "Jamie's a freshman halfback."

Mary's laughter was high-pitched and pleasant— just shy of a giggle. Staring directly into O'Hare's eyes, she said, "Who rushed for three thousand yards in his senior year at Wilkes-Barre High School. Who was named Pennsylvania's player of the year twice. Who is sidelined for his freshman year because of an Achilles-tendon tear, which explains why he's in here the night before a game."

O'Hare clapped a hand to his forehead and rolled his eyes upward. Why was every one of his gestures so letter perfect? Rudy wondered bitterly.

O'Hare said, "Have I just died and gone to heaven? Come on, Mary McDonough, what's with the biography? How did you know all that stuff?"

"Easy. I'm the world's biggest Notre Dame football fan."

That was more than Rudy could take. "Hey, I thought *I* was," he said.

They both ignored him, their eyes fixed on each other. They were caught up in that wonderful first moment of mutual physical attraction.

"Actually," O'Hare told her, "I'm having dinner with my brother and his wife over in the corner. Would you like to join us?"

"Sure," said Mary. She rose from the stool and pushed her hair back from her forehead. She and Jamie O'Hare had that in common, Rudy thought—the small and perfect gesture. Was it something you inherited like money or brains, or did you have to practice for hours in front of a mirror? With a brief glance at Rudy, she said, "See you later."

Before Rudy could even reply—he was reaching for something witty—they were gone. He stood there following their progress across the crowded room and tried not to let his sadness show. The fact that they were obviously made for each other—by background, by physical beauty—did nothing to ease the pain. Still staring after them, he drank down his beer in a long gulp, picked up the other one, and carried it to the bar. Three or four beers and an hour or so later, he said to the bartender, "Is that Bob Gladieux over there?"

"Yeah. Another beer?"

"Oh man, that Gladieux, he was a great one, wasn't he? Remember in 1966 against Michigan State? Man, what a game that was—the greatest. We're number one, they're number two. Nick Eddy was hurt and Hanratty got wiped out early in the game and then

George Goeddeke sprained his ankle. But Gladieux, he was great. He scored the only touchdown we made, and considering all the injuries, it's lucky we got out of that game with a ten-ten tie, don't you think? A lot of people've called it the game of the century."

"A beer or not?" said the bartender, giving the counter an angry swipe with his cloth. He didn't know which he hated more, college sports or college kids. He'd pretty much made up his mind to return to the River Rouge plant in Detroit and put some Fords together. College kids!

At that moment Mary walked by, and in an effort to stand, Rudy nearly slid off his stool. "Hey—Mary, Mary, quite contrary. How does your garden grow? You have a good time with good ol' Prince? Mr. Golden Boy?" His speech was slurred and he realized he'd had a couple too many.

She stopped and frowned at him. Even her frown was breathtakingly beautiful; he could easily take that frown for a lifetime. "Are you all right?" she said.

Trying to hide the slur and clutching to the counter for support, he said, "I'm great—really. I just wanted to say, I wanted to tell you, it's great working with you, Mary. Terrific."

"Thanks," she said. But there was no answering smile, only concern.

"You said you were the biggest Notre Dame football fan in the world. It's funny, I always thought I was. So we really have this bond, don't we? This thing in common."

Mary nodded and started to leave, but Rudy held her with his voice, saying, "In fact I'm gonna be playing for the Irish next fall. I've talked to Coach Parseghian about it and—well, the thing is, I'm at Holy Cross for a semester, maybe two. Father Cavanaugh promised if I make the grades, I'll have a good chance of getting in. More than a good chance—I'll *be* in. And so far, for the first time in my life, my grades have been great, so—"

"You aren't a student at Notre Dame?" Mary cut in.

"Well, like I'm telling you right now—as of this moment not officially. But next semester, for sure, I will be."

Mary shook her head. "Then you can't be part of the Boosters."

"Come on, Mary, just pretend you don't know my situation. Can't you do that? Bend the rules a little for a fellow Notre Dame football nut? You know I'm the biggest fan in the world—next to you, of course." He tried to duplicate O'Hare's sophisticated bow and nearly staggered into Mary.

"It's the rules," she said. "Somebody makes them, I follow them. Maybe you should try that." She turned away and disappeared through the door. Rudy, heavy with pain, plumped down on his stool, his head in his hands.

"Shit," he said. "I'm screwing up left and right."

The bartender studied him impassively. The kid didn't act like a college kid, which as far as the bartender was concerned was a plus. He seemed like guys he'd worked with on assembly lines in Detroit and Lansing. In a little friendlier tone, he said, "Another beer?"

"Yeah. Why not?"

"You can't live with 'em, you can't live without 'em," the bartender observed.

"Yeah, ain't that the truth," said Rudy, looking up and smiling sadly. He extended his arm across the counter. "Name's Rudy Ruettiger."

"Buddy Fuller," said the bartender. "Glad to mee-cha."

"Buddy, I'm gonna stick around here for a while. Just keep the beers comin' until I can't find my mouth with the glass, then kick me the hell out."

The next day, Saturday, was game day, complete with all the color, pomp, and circumstance of the most tradition-rich college-football program in the country. By late morning, the fields surrounding the stadium were transformed into a boisterous beehive of pre-game tailgating. Fans dressed in blue and gold or wearing body paint—many of the older alumni sporting their trademark plaid pants—kept warm with hamburgers or hot dogs grilled off the backs of the cars and washed down with generous quantities of whiskey and gin and beer. Other alumni and students, all pumped up for the first game of the 1972 season, stood outside in large festive groups or streamed into the stadium. Wandering among those well-scrubbed, ebullient masses was Rudy, looking disheveled, a bit frantic, and suffering from a brutal hangover. He clutched a ten-dollar bill in his hand and announced in a loud voice, "One ticket. I need one ticket. Anybody got one ticket to sell? Please, anybody, I really need one ticket!"

People steered a wide berth around him, doing their best to render him invisible. Suddenly he felt a hand press down, not so gently, on his shoulder. He looked up into the blue, Irish eyes of a policeman, who stared at his money, and then said, "Number one, ten bucks is about ninety short of what you need—*if* you can find a seller, which I doubt. Number two, this is Notre Dame, not just any old college. Anybody shows up here holding a ticket is not looking to sell it. And number three—most important—you better vamoose now before I run you in."

Rudy nodded, started to say something, then decided that silence might be the best policy. He walked away. Once he was out of sight of the policeman, he strolled casually toward a ticket booth on the opposite side of the stadium. There were only a scattering of people still outside of the stadium, and Rudy could hear the rising and falling roar of the spectators inside, the thumping beat of the band, and then the sonorous sound of the PA's player introductions. On the outside again, he thought. It was the most important game of his life and he wasn't going to see a single play, be a part of the excitement, and have memories to store away forever. He wouldn't be with the kids in the student section linked arm in arm, swaying in unison as they sang "Alma Mater" (Notre Dame Our Mother), accompanied by the band. Rudy had been told that it was one of the most touching moments you could ever hope to experience, that many kids cried, not out of sadness but from happiness at the pride they felt in being a part of it all. And he was missing it—once again on the outside looking in.

Rudy's eyes darted around as he desperately tried to figure out some way to pass through the turnstiles and get into the stadium. He couldn't come this far and be stymied; it was unacceptable, completely un-fair. There just *had* to be a way to get in!

The Irish kick off, the PA announced, *and defend the north goal.*

As the band blasted out the school song Rudy walked up to a ticket taker and, shouting over the pan-demonium from inside the stadium, said, "I have to see the game. Do you understand me? I *have* to. It's life and death. I've come all this way, from Joliet—oh, forget about that, from the other side of the world—I've waited all my life for this, and all I've got is ten bucks. Isn't there any way, don't you have it in your heart to let me in? I'm sure there's a couple feet of space I could squeeze into."

The ticket taker's expression was set in stone. "If you don't leave right now," he said, "I'll call a secur-ity guard."

"Thanks," said Rudy. "Thanks a lot, buddy."

"Get lost."

As the booming drums reached their crescendo in preparation for kickoff, Rudy turned and walked away.

Early the next morning, Fortune and Rudy set wheelbarrows of sod down on the field. Fortune pulled a sod patch off the top and dropped to his knees, grunting. "Man, this field sure took some beatin'," he said. "Good thing the team didn't get beat themselves."

Rudy looked around the stadium, littered with de-bris from the afternoon before, and said, "Fortune, did you see Eric Penick's kickoff return?"

"Nope. Don't watch the sport. Fishin' is my speed."

"You don't know what you're missing. I saw it on TV," said Rudy. "He broke free about here." Pretending he was holding the ball, cradling it against his chest, he started running down the field. "And Penick breaks a tackle," Rudy yelled in the husky, excited tones of a radio announcer. "He's off to the races. Can anybody catch him? No! He's on to the forty, the thirty, the twenty, the ten—*touchdown!*" Standing in the end zone, wearing a wide grin, Rudy held up his hands signaling a touchdown.

"Hey, we got work to do," said Fortune.

Rudy ran back. "Have you ever seen a game here?"

"Nope. I told you, I'm not much for the sport."

"Then your first game will be when you come to see me play."

"If you say so, kid. Now, you gonna watch me or help me?"

Rudy got down on his knees and started tamping new sod into the ground. "Fortune," he said, without looking up.

"Yeah?"

"I don't mind telling you, I never felt lower than I did yesterday. It was a real bummer not being able to see the game. I felt like shit, to be honest."

Fortune was listening as he worked but did not reply.

"Then I went to the bar and watched the game, and that really spooked me."

"What spooked you?"

"Notre Dame won, Penick made the great run back.

Clements was terrific, they all were—but you know what? I was *still* in the dumps. That's never happened to me before. The Irish could always make me feel like a million dollars, win or lose. Especially win. But not this time."

"I guess you're growing up, kid. Life ain't always easy and games can't solve your problems."

"Yeah, but then I went back to the maintenance shed," said Rudy, still not looking up, but aware that Fortune had turned to look at him. "I wanted to tell you before—about how great you made me feel. The blankets and everything. The food and all. And then last night there was a key so I wouldn't have to climb through the window like a thief. And more food . . ." Rudy looked up at Fortune, who was now very busily hunched over his sod. "Fortune—you made me feel good again. Good about everything. Okay, I didn't see the game. So what? There'll be other games. The important thing is, I got you for a friend. What I'm trying to say is, thank you, but I'm stumbling all over the place. Just a klutz, I guess."

"Don't know what you're talkin' about," said Fortune. "That maintenance shed is university property. I keep that cot in there for my back condition."

"But, Fortune—"

"You hear what I just said?" Fortune glared at Rudy. "I don't know nothin' about nothin'. You understand?"

Rudy stared at Fortune and nodded. When he returned to work, a slow smile spread over his face.

Near the end of the school year, when the warm weather at last arrived in South Bend, came the Irish festival *AnTostal,* which Rudy had been long awaiting. For three wonderful days the campus went crazy, with basketball tourneys, tugs-of-war, chariot races, outdoor carnivals, picnics, and just general hell raising. All the students—including Rudy—saw *AnTostal* as the last escape before the tension of finals set in, and thus they enjoyed it to the fullest.

And for Rudy, the tension of final exams was especially great, because riding on those exams was the fulfillment of his oldest and most cherished dream— entering Notre Dame.

Entering in the fall of 1973.

He pored feverishly over his notes, his books. He worked with D-Bob. He went without sleep, he ate very little.

I'm going to get in, I'm going to get in, he kept telling himself, and there was no sacrifice too great for that.

12

When Rudy went home for the summer he waited for the letter from Notre Dame. He was all psyched up; he just *knew* they had to accept him because he'd pulled down just about the top grades in his class at Holy Cross, and he was taking parallel courses with the Notre Dame freshmen. Also, they knew his history—coming from the steel mills, four years out of high school, and trying to do the impossible and succeeding. He sweated out the wait for that letter of acceptance, telling his parents and his old friends around Joliet that in the fall of '73 he'd be a Notre Dame student. In fact he told some of his friends he had already been accepted.

Then, one hot June day, he came home from the mill (as much as he hated it, he had decided to return there for the summer to earn money for the following year's tuition) and his mother handed him an envelope. It was a thin envelope and that worried him.

Good news usually meant a thick envelope full of questionnaires, catalogs, and forms to process. Standing there in the kitchen, he tore the envelope open and his eyes raced right to the words *We are sorry to inform you* and he sank into a chair and began to cry. His mother held his head against her breast and wept along with him. "It's like dyin', Ma," he said when he could bring himself to speak. "The pain is just awful."

That night he borrowed Danilo's car and drove straight through to South Bend. His plan was to go directly to the president of Notre Dame, Father Hesburgh, and ask him point-blank why he would do something so unthinkable to him and his family, why would Hesburgh try to kill his dream. Who deserved the chance at a Notre Dame education more than he did? Who had worked as hard and showed as much dedication?

As it happened, Father Hesburgh was away on business and Rudy found Father Cavanaugh in Corby Hall. They walked together around campus late that evening and it was all Rudy could do to contain his tears.

"I'm proud of you," said Father Cavanaugh, reaching out to touch Rudy on the arm. "I know how hard you worked for those grades."

"But no matter how hard I work, I'm never gonna get in," said Rudy. "That's kind of obvious, isn't it?"

Father Cavanaugh shrugged. "I couldn't say. I'm not on the admissions committee."

Rudy looked at him. "What if you were?"

"That's an easy answer," said the priest. "You're in."

"Maybe my dad was right," said Rudy. "Maybe I don't belong here. I've always thought the point of life is to stretch yourself to the limit—but maybe I've overreached."

Father Cavanaugh said quietly, "One of the best things about you is your toughness, your resilience, Rudy. You mustn't start feeling sorry for yourself. It never helps you to achieve your goals."

"If Holy Cross is all there is," said Rudy, "I don't see the point."

Father Cavanaugh walked on, expressionless, and then said finally, "My advice is, go home. Let yourself heal and think very carefully about your next step. Don't make a snap decision. Remember—you can always return to Holy Cross for your sophomore year and try for Notre Dame again. They'll take you as a junior."

"Do you think that's what I should do?"

Father Cavanaugh shook his head. "I can't make that decision for you. I can't lead your life." The priest hesitated. "But I would suggest that you try very hard not to give up. Don't ever forget that perseverance has gotten you this far. Who knows how much further it can take you?"

Fortune was sitting on a bench taking a break on the grounds outside the stadium. Rudy spotted him and slowly walked over, trying to force a smile and then giving up on it.

"You're one sad-lookin' kid," said Fortune. "Shoulders all slumped like some old geezer. I guess you didn't make it, huh?"

"Total failure," Rudy answered. "Everything I did,

the work, the studying, four hours' sleep a night—for nothing.''

Fortune sipped on a Coke and stared straight ahead. Rudy snuck a look at his friend and was surprised, and hurt, that he didn't seem particularly concerned or sympathetic.

''What I mean is, I've blown another year of eligibility.'' He pounded the bench with his fist. ''This whole year's been a waste.''

Fortune turned to Rudy, his lips tight, his nostrils flaring. ''Waste? Is that all you can say?''

''I didn't get in. That's the bottom line.''

''No, sir. Wrong. It ain't the bottom line. You got your head so far up your ass about that damn football team and wearing the blue and gold you don't get the fact you just got one year of top-quality education. Waste? Those Holy Cross teachers helpin' you, D-Bob helpin' you? *Waste?* You talk like that, you come around cryin' and feelin' sorry for yourself, you be wastin' *my* time.''

Fortune stood and walked away. Rudy looked after him, surprised at the outburst but, curiously, feeling less unhappy than he had since the moment he'd opened the letter the day before.

The next few days, back home in Joliet, were some of the most painful of Rudy's life. Danilo planned a big barbecue that Saturday, the day Rudy returned from Notre Dame. His mother had promised not to tell Danilo the news; Rudy wanted to break it to the old man himself, in his own words, not through Ma. She always made excuses for him, tried to protect him from Danilo's anger. Early that afternoon Rudy sat in the den with Frank and Danilo, drinking beer and watching the Cubs on TV. A large contingent of the Ruettiger clan was over for the day, and Mark, a rambunctious eight-year-old nephew of Rudy's, grabbed his arm.

"Where you been so long, Unc?"

"Going to college at Holy Cross," said Rudy, picking the boy up on his lap.

Mark grabbed a handful of Rudy's jacket. "If you're going to Holy Cross, how come you got this on?"

"Because I'm going to school there—not next year but the year after. I have one year to go at Holy Cross." So the decision was made, just like that, in response to an eight-year-old nephew's casual question. He would go back and try again to be admitted to Notre Dame. He wouldn't give up.

"If you go to Notre Dame, I'm going there, too," said Mark.

"Yeah, me, too," said Mark's ten-year-old brother, Bernie.

Danilo, during a commercial break, turned his attention to Rudy. "So your ma tells me you got good grades."

"Two A's and three B's," said Rudy.

"Good for you. Easy subjects? Is that it?"

"No, Pop. Hard subjects. I studied very hard for those grades."

"Good for you." Danilo nodded, but his eyes were once again glued to the game. Ron Santo drilled a double into the left-field corner, knocking in a run, and Danilo grunted with pleasure. "Some sweet swing, that Santo," he said.

"Hey, bro, you gonna do the barbecue with us to-night?" said Frank.

"Yeah. Why?"

"The kid's got a hell of a surprise waiting for him, doesn't he, Pop?" Frank winked at his father.

"What kind of surprise?" Rudy asked his older brother.

"Just wait and see."

"Hey, Frank, I haven't heard the good word from you. What do you think of my grades? I'll bet you didn't think your little brother had it in him. Couldn't cut the old mustard, right? Isn't that what you thought?"

"We're all proud as punch," Frank said dryly. "Now we got the Cubbies and Cards here in a tie, ninth inning, all right? We gotta keep that fuckin' Brock off the bases."

"Watch your language, Frankie," said Danilo absently.

Rudy knelt beside his father and, angling away from Frank, said, "I didn't get in, Pop."

Danilo slowly shifted his eyes away from the TV and focused on Rudy. "What?"

"Notre Dame turned me down for next year." Rudy tried to read his father's expression.

"Well," said Danilo, "I hope you get what you want. I always told you that was some kind of impossible dream. But you wouldn't listen. Not your stubborn self."

"Are you disappointed?"

Danilo was staring at the game again. "Naw. Like I say, I never gave you a chance in hell of gettin' in."

Rudy swallowed his growing anger. He said, "I'll get in when I'm a junior. Trust me I will."

"Yeah," said Danilo.

"You don't believe me, do you?"

"If you say so."

"I saw every home game this season, except the first one. I thought about you every minute I was there, about how much you would love it."

"Shit," Danilo said to Frank, "can't we throw anybody out on the bases?"

"That Brock is quick," said Frank. "You walk him, it's a double guaranteed."

"You've got to come over for a game next fall," said Rudy. "It's the most exciting thing you can ever imagine. You know, being there. Seeing the players in person. The band, the crowd singing. Everything."

His eyes still glued to the TV, Danilo said, "Watching the games here on TV's just fine with me. I don't need the crowd. All the bullshit."

"But it's so much more exciting when you're there, Pop." He took a deep breath. "Would you come to a game if I was playing?"

"Jesus," said Frank, disgusted. "We still have to hear this crap."

"I wasn't talking to you, Frank."

"A year of junior college sure hasn't made you any smarter, little bro."

"Drop the little-bro stuff," said Rudy. "Just drop it."

Danilo finally turned to Rudy. "I'm glad you made good grades," he said. "Sometimes you don't seem like a Ruettiger and maybe that's not so bad." He shot

a look at Frank and said, "Lay off him," then turned
back to the set.

"Hey, Rudy."

Rudy turned to see Johnny and Sherry standing in
the doorway to the den, smiling and holding hands.
He was shocked; for a moment he thought he was
only imagining they were standing there. Until that instant when he saw them together, Rudy had believed
he felt nothing for Sherry, that their relationship was
dead, buried and in the past. But seeing her with his
brother filled him with a deep hurt, a feeling of be-
trayal. Suddenly he realized that he'd depended on
Sherry being there if he ever needed her, that if all
else failed he could return to her and pick up where
they'd left off, that she was his security blanket in a
way. He tried to stay calm and to smile, but it was a
faltering gesture; he was aware that the others' eyes
were on him.

Johnny let go of Sherry's hand, walked over, and
put his arm around Rudy. "How you doing?" he said.

"Fine, Johnny. And you?" He forced himself not
to look at Sherry; he didn't trust his emotions.

"Just great. And listen, I just want to tell you—
your going to college . . . well, I think it's great."

"Thanks," said Rudy. "I appreciate that."

With a quick glance at Danilo and Frank, Johnny
said, "Some of us never had the guts or support to
pull it off. I'm really happy you did."

Neither Danilo nor Frank seemed to hear; they were
concentrating on the baseball action on TV.

Johnny said to Sherry, "I'll be in the kitchen. I
could use a drink. A stiff one."

Johnny squeezed Rudy's shoulder and left the den.

Rudy finally felt able to look at Sherry (she was doing her hair differently now, more natural, like the Notre Dame girls), then quickly shifted his eyes away and walked into the hallway. After a moment's hesitation she followed.

"Rudy . . ." She reached out to touch his hand.

"It's okay, Sherry. Don't say anything."

"I'm sorry. I should've written you."

"Well, neither of us did much writing."

"This is no way to find out, though. I feel responsible."

"It doesn't matter. You don't owe me anything."

She touched his cheek lightly with her fingers. "You may not believe me, but I hope you make it. I really hope you get everything you want. Notre Dame, football, all your dreams come true." She smiled at him. "Do you have a girlfriend?"

"No."

"Well, I also hope you find the girl of your dreams."

"Thanks, Sherry. And take good care of my brother."

Her smile grew wider. "Believe me, Rudy, he takes good care of me."

Rudy glanced into the den. Both Danilo and Frank were watching them, and when they saw Rudy staring at them, they quickly turned away. Rudy pushed the front door open and left the house. Danilo struggled out of the BarcaLounger, crossed the room, and watched Rudy walk down the street, his hands stuffed deep in his pockets, his head bowed.

"Kids," he whispered as he watched his son walk out of sight. He shook his head and sighed.

PART

FOUR

★

1974

13

Rudy had never been particularly religious and had always taken Catholicism—and God—for granted. They existed like the trees and the sea, but they had never affected his life on a daily basis—or so it had been when he was younger. But Pete's death marked the beginning of a change in Rudy's thinking. God came right up close on that awful day, got in his face, and took his best friend to heaven. At first Rudy had not visited the Grotto at Notre Dame, but religious belief pervaded the campus and he knew that many students would visit the Grotto and fall to their knees before an important test, praying for divine intervention. The Grotto was a refuge for many during desperate times. School problems, love problems, parent problems drew students—and some faculty, too— to the Grotto. A replica of a shrine to the Virgin Mary in Lourdes, France, and resembling a cave, it sat near St. Mary's Lake and was a place of peace, of peace and hope, and it possessed a reverent, soothing, and mysterious ambience that inspired a lot of students. It inspired Rudy now. He stuffed a dollar into a box, lit a candle, and knelt and prayed.

"Lord," he began, "let me start out with a little history here. Oh, I know you're familiar with my story—you know everybody's story—but you have so many people to attend to. Billions. I came here in the fall of 1972 hoping to get into Notre Dame, but I wasn't anywhere near prepared. So I got a chance to attend Holy Cross Junior College, where I still am. I'm in my second year here now, and at first I couldn't cut Holy Cross, either. It was high school all over again; so much stuff I couldn't understand. But I was blessed with a lot of good friends—D-Bob and Father Cavanaugh, I'm sure he talks to you often, and Fortune who keeps me on track and others—and they helped me through the rough times. But then, in the spring of seventy-three, just a year ago now, I came here and prayed. I prayed harder than I've ever prayed in my life—but not half as hard as I'm praying today. I prayed that Notre Dame would accept me in my sophomore year. I'd ended up my first semester with two A's and three B's, much better than a three-point average and way beyond my wildest dreams. But they didn't take me.

"Now this is my last chance." He squeezed his eyes tight shut, concentrating on his prayer. "You know Notre Dame doesn't take transfers in the senior year, so it's now or never for me, Lord. I've worked so hard, I've given everything I've got—I believe I've earned the chance. . . ." Rudy reached into his pocket and removed five ten-dollar bills and stuffed them into the box. He knelt again before fifty lit candles. "I guess you could call this raising the ante. I know you can't buy miracles, but I'm so desperate, I want this so much. I know my grades went down a little this term, but I had all these different extracurricular activities, plus three straight victories in Bengal bouts. I've made a little reputation for myself there. A lot of the football players know me by name now and we hang out together. But Father Cavanaugh has warned me not to raise my hopes too high. He says these admissions people are a funny bunch, that you can't predict what they're gonna do. But, Lord, they'll listen to you. And I'm praying you'll put in a good word for me. And if you do, I'll promise this—I'll pledge my heart and soul to doing the very best I can possibly do—in the classroom, on the team. I'll do everything in my power to prove myself worthy. . . ."

He heard footsteps and looked up to see Father Cavanaugh standing over him, a concerned look on his face. He inclined his head toward the candles and said, "How much did this conflagration cost you?"

"Fifty bucks. Most of my savings." Rudy tried to force a smile. "I'm desperate."

Father Cavanaugh put a hand on Rudy's shoulder. "I know."

"If I don't get in next semester, it's over, dead. Notre Dame doesn't take senior transfers."

"Well, you've done a hell of a job trying to chase down your dream." Father Cavanaugh looked up, clasped his hands over his chest, and smiled. "Excuse my language, Lord."

"I don't care what kind of job I've done, Father. If it doesn't produce results, it doesn't mean anything."

"Oh, I think you'll discover it will."

Rudy stared at the burning candles. "Maybe I haven't prayed enough."

"I'm sure that's not a problem," said the priest. "Praying is something we do in our time. But the answers come in God's time. We have no control over that. It's important to be patient and leave yourself in His hands. Now go home, relax." Father Cavanaugh grabbed Rudy by the arm, assisted him to his feet, and started walking him away from the altar.

"Is there anything else I can do?" said Rudy. He looked beseechingly at the priest, his eyes red-rimmed from lack of sleep. "Can you help me?"

"Son, in the thirty-five years of my life devoted to religious studies, I've come up with only two hard, incontrovertible facts."

Rudy looked at him, waiting for him to continue.

"There is a God," Father Cavanaugh said slowly. "And I'm not Him."

The next morning Rudy arrived at the student mail center having tossed and turned all night. The letter he had been waiting for—and dreading—was in his box. He stared at it. Was it thick enough this time? He wasn't sure. He stared at it, unable to breathe, unable to open it. He stuck it in his pocket and walked over to St. Joseph's Lake. He sat on a bench and stared at the rowboats full of kids who seemed impossibly relaxed, at the swans and ducks, but he saw everything through the dark, distorted vision of fear. He took a deep breath, closed his eyes, and opened the letter. "I promise," he said out loud, "that I will never ask for anything ever again."

He opened his eyes. The first words that caught his

eyes were . . . *Congratulations. You have been admit-ted to the University of Notre Dame.* . . .

He jumped up from the bench, spread his arms toward the sky, and yelled, "Oh, my God—I really *did* it. *I did it. I really did it.*" He jumped, clicked his heels in the air, and ran as fast as he could to the maintenance shed to find Fortune.

The grounds keeper shook his head. "I knew you had it in you, kid."

He found D-Bob over a plate of hamburgers and fries at the Huddle.

"Got in, D-Bob," he said, waving the letter in his friend's face. He grabbed a fry from D-Bob's plate, swallowed it, and grinned. D-Bob embraced him and said, "Atta boy, Gipper. Now you can get to be a big football star and we'll have the pick of the girls."

At five o'clock the next morning, Rudy borrowed Fortune's van and drove straight through to Joliet. He went directly to the mill, to Danilo's office. Danilo and a number of his coworkers, including Frank, were drinking coffee and gearing up for the day's work ahead. Rudy burst in, ran over to his father, waving his arms and grinning maniacally.

"What's wrong?" said Danilo, trying to push up from his chair.

Rudy stuck the letter under his father's nose. "Read it," he said.

Danilo put on his reading glasses and slowly read the letter, pronouncing each word under his breath. When he finished, he removed his glasses and looked at his son. He shook his head and the beginnings of a smile hovered on his lips. "This is really something, Rudy. I gotta say it. This is really something."

"I did it," said Rudy.

Danilo nodded. "You did it."

They stared at each other with considerable emotion, but neither made a move toward the other.

Danilo turned to his coworkers and yelled, "Hey, my son's going to Notre Dame. How about that? Ain't that somethin'?"

They surrounded Rudy, many of them having known him since he was a child; they congratulated him, pounded him on the back, pumped his hand. Rudy spotted Frank seated at a control panel, staring at him with an expression impossible to read. Rudy went over to him and held out the acceptance letter.

"Want to read it?"

"I'll take your word," said Frank. "You got in." He barely glanced at the letter and handed it back to Rudy.

"Can you believe it, Frank?"

"I never thought you'd pull it off. But you did. So—what can I say? Good for you. You're a better man than I thought you were." He looked away from Rudy's smiling face and returned to his work.

"I have to get back right away, Pop," Rudy said to Danilo.

"What's your hurry? You just got here. You can't even stay for dinner? We got to celebrate. It ain't every day a Ruettiger gets into Notre Dame."

"Football practice starts this week," said Rudy. He snuck a look at Frank and grinned; his older brother looked quickly away. "Now I'm eligible, Pop. I finally got my chance, and it's up to me now."

14

Coach Warren posed, hands on hips, in front of about forty walk-on hopefuls of varying sizes and talents but all with a single goal in mind: to beat the long odds and be one of the lucky five who would survive a week of bone-crushing drills, prove their grit to the coaches, and make the team. Rudy, one of the forty, stood at the head of the group, as close to Coach Warren as he could get, bouncing on his toes anxiously and listening hard, afraid he might miss something. The regular team was practicing on the field behind the walk-ons, and they were wearing the traditional blue-and-gold uniforms, not the walk-on gray.

"Let me tell it to you as plain as I can," Coach Warren shouted so that all could hear. "We have ninety-five players here so accomplished as athletes in high school we gave them full scholarships to the best football program in the country. And I mean the *best*. NCAA regulations allow us to dress just sixty for home games, which means at least thirty scholarship players are going to be watching from the stands. So if any of you have any fantasies about running out of the stadium tunnel with your gold helmet shining in the sun, I have some advice for you. Leave your fantasies right here.

"Of you forty dreamers out there, we have room for maybe five of you—if we can find five of you with even an ounce of talent. And my job is not for you to like me. Let's get that straight right now. And you're not *going* to like me, I can guarantee that. My job is to work you hard for five days. Whoever is standing and breathing at the end we may use for our scout teams. You lucky ones'll be running the opposition's plays week in and week out. You're dispensable, you got it? Our first team will pound on you like you're their worst enemies.

"Have I scared any of you? Have I dashed some dreams? If any of you answer yes to either question, leave now and don't waste my time. The rest of you, let's get to work. . . ."

On the very first drill, Rudy was in the center of a pileup trying to make a tackle. His face made direct and forceful contact with an opposing lineman's knee; he got up dripping blood and feeling a numbness blanket his jaw, but he waved off a towel offered by a coach's assistant and eagerly lined up for the next drill, fire in his eyes, ready to give his all.

As the first practice continued, the drills got increasingly tougher. Rudy put forth a relentless effort, aware that Coach Yonto, Ara Parseghian's principal aide, was observing the walk-ons. Yonto was fascinated by Rudy's nonstop motion and his total willingness to absorb the hardest shots and come back for more. In a "hamburger drill," Rudy was sandwiched between two tackles and was stunned by a crunching blow to his chest and stomach, but he simply sucked wind and forced a grin as though to say, "Is that the best you can do?" and hopped to his feet for more.

On the sidelines, Yonto pointed out Rudy to Coach Warren. Warren frowned and shook his head as though to say, "*That kid?* He's less than nothin'."

In another drill, Rudy tried to rush the passer through two offensive linemen, both built like behemoths. Even though he had no chance, he still hurled his body fearlessly forward. He could live with the pain, and after the first hour of drills, it covered every inch of his body; what he couldn't live with was not making the team. When he got up from the ground, he was half bent over, holding his ribs, his eyes bloodshot and swollen, his jersey torn and bloody.

"I'll get you pussies next time," he yelled, and some of his walk-on teammates joined him in laughter.

Coach Warren blew a whistle. "Okay," he yelled. "Relax for a few minutes." He stared at the ragged group, shook his head, and walked over to Yonto. "What I'd like to do, I'd like to get rid of them all," he said.

Each night during that week's tryouts, Rudy went back to the maintenance shed and soaked his shoulders and knees and thumbs in ice. Those five days nearly shattered his confidence that he could play Notre Dame football. The West Point drill, the Bull in the Ring, the Foreman Shiver drill (which was the worst because all of the linemen were waiting to tee

off on you) inflicted pain on every muscle and joint of
an intensity he had never before experienced. But his
desire always won over his uncertainty. He considered
every hit he took, every slight from guys like O'Hare
simply as obstacles he had to be man enough to rise
above. They were trying to steal his dream and he
wouldn't let them do that. He *couldn't* let them do
that. He would die first.

At the end of the final day of tryouts, Coach Yonto
approached Coach Warren. "The kid with blood all
over his jersey. What's his story? His size and all, he
could pass for a kid from the Pop Warner Football
League."

"Ruettiger? What a joke. No athletic skills. The
guy is pathetic."

"Maybe," said Yonto. "But I've been watching
him all week. He puts out more effort than any two
guys we got combined. It's always good to have a
why-can't-you-bust-your-butt-like-me? kind of guy
around. They inspire the others."

Warren waved a hand dismissively. "If it's the right
guy, yeah, but believe me, Joe, this shrimp is not the
right guy. He can kamikaze all he wants, but he lacks
the basic skills."

"Hmm," said Yonto, still looking skeptical.

Warren turned back to the walk-ons and blew his
whistle. "Practice is officially over now, fellas. We
had a fine week, and thanks for coming out. Shower
up and we'll let you know who's sticking."

Rudy, looking like a serious accident victim, got
dressed gingerly. He ached from the top of his head to
his toes. Jim Obsetnick, a handsome junior who

seemed to wear a perpetual frown, dressed next to him in silence.

"Think you made the team?" Rudy asked.

Obsetnick slowly turned and glowered at him. "Unfortunately," he said.

Rudy was so flabbergasted he forgot his pain for a moment. "I don't get you. What's so unfortunate about making the team?"

Obsetnick's expression softened a little as he looked Rudy over; the guy was so small and so incredibly banged up. He'd seen him running around all week like a maniac, taking hits and taking more hits, and he figured the poor guy was a little off his rocker. "It's my third year as a walk-on," he said, "and I've never dressed for a game. I had scholarships to two Big Ten schools, but my father was an All-American here. Family pressure, you know. I didn't have much of a choice."

"You've never been cut," said Rudy, "so you still have a chance. That's the way I'd look at it."

Obsetnick's sour expression vanished for a moment and he broke into a soft chuckle. "Chance to play? You got to be joking. The only reason they keep me here is because I'm a legacy. This place loves legacies. But when it comes to the reality—the game and who gets to play it—I'm no more valuable than a tackling dummy."

"Well, I'd give anything to be in your shoes, to get a shot," said Rudy.

"Well, you know what they say, don't you? Don't wish for something too hard, you might get it."

"I don't think I've heard that saying," said Rudy. "And I don't believe it—"

"Ruettiger!"

Rudy froze, then turned to see Coach Yonto at the door; he motioned to Rudy by wiggling his index finger.

Shirttail flapping, his shoes untied, eyes wide and heart pumping, Rudy ran over to the coach.

"Come on," said Coach Yonto, "let's take a walk."

"Can't think of anything else I'd rather do," said Rudy, hobbling along beside the older man. Shaking with fear, with anticipation, with the beginnings of hope.

"You want on the team pretty bad, don't you?" said the coach.

"Bad? Yeah, Coach. But bad doesn't describe it. I don't have the vocabulary."

"You sure busted your balls over the last five days," said Yonto.

"I'll do anything to make the team."

Coach Yonto strolled along through the cool spring air, his hands clasped behind his back, seemingly deep in thought. Then: "You think you can give me the same kind of effort day in and day out for the next five months?" he said.

"Sir, there is no question—absolutely no question."

"You say that now, but you don't know the realities of being a walk-on. It's dirty grub work. No glory, no visibility. You get kicked in the ass, you eat dirt. You play against the guys who are starters, guys who hate the idea of taking a shot from some scrimmage guy. They double-team you and beat up on you. Those are the realities."

"I understand. I'm prepared for that."

"Some of the guys will trip you, blindside you, kick you in the jewels. They'll hit you like a freight train. Can you handle that? Can you take all the shit that goes with being a walk-on?"

"I can take it," said Rudy. "That's what I'm here for. This isn't all that bad, you know. I've worked in the steel mills."

Coach Yonto nodded. "Well," he said slowly, "I'll tell you one thing right now. If you let up so much as a hair, I'll throw your butt off the team so fast you won't know what hit you."

Rudy looked at him, stunned, his mouth open. "Off the team? Did you say off the team? That means first I have to be *on* the team, right?"

"Don't let me down," said the coach.

Rudy did a painful little jig as he continued to stare at Coach Yonto. "I'm on the team, right? Am I actually on the team?"

Yonto studied Rudy and wondered if he was making a mistake with this kid. He was too short to be a football player; he wasn't very fast; he wasn't very skillful—but he wanted it so badly. That was the quality that intrigued Yonto. He had never worked with a player who wanted something as badly as this kid did. "Yeah, Ruettiger," he said, "that's what I've been saying. You're on the team."

Rudy let out a yell, a war whoop, and hugged Coach Yonto.

"Hey, hey, hey," said the coach, backing away.

"I'm on the team," said Rudy. "I made the team. *I made the team! I made the team!*" he sang as he ran around in circles.

Yonto watched him and grinned. "Kid, I knew you were crazy. Any guy willing to take a hit like you do, he's got to be crazy."

"Of *course* I'm crazy," Rudy yelled. "Otherwise I'd be workin' in the mill in Joliet, Illinois, with all my sane relatives."

Later that day, when he heard the news about Father Cavanaugh from D-Bob, Rudy rushed straight to the priest's office.

"This morning, Father, I gave you terrific news," he said, "and now this. I mean this is the worst news I've ever heard."

"No, it isn't, Rudy. Not for me it isn't."

"But you can't leave here."

Father Cavanaugh laughed. "I can't? Who says I can't?"

"It's just that I finally get into Notre Dame—two long, hard years and I'd never have done it without you. And I'm gonna be here for two more years. I can't tell you how tough it'll be without you."

"You mustn't be selfish," the priest said softly. "Be happy for me."

"I am—but I still feel miserable. I can't help it."

Father Cavanaugh put a hand on Rudy's shoulder. "You'll do just fine. Believe me, you will. By the way, no more sleeping in the maintenance office. You have a job in the seminary, where you'll have your own room. I told you I'd swing that for you, didn't I?"

"Thanks, Father, I really appreciate it. But I still don't understand. Why do you have to leave?"

Father Cavanaugh seemed to ponder the question.

He removed his glasses, rubbed them absently on his sleeve, then replaced them. "It wasn't easy for me to become a priest," he said. "I fought a lot of battles, mostly in here." He pointed to his head and his heart. "When I was assigned to Notre Dame, I thought I'd achieved everything I'd worked for. And my years here have been the most pleasurable of my life."

"Then why? Why do you have to leave?"

"It's almost been *too* pleasurable. I've gotten a little soft. In fact, in the last two years you've been reminding me of something I've lost along the way."

"Me?"

"You've got a warrior's spirit, Rudy," said Father Cavanaugh. "You're a fighter, a battler. It's what makes you alive in your whole being. You've taught me something about life, and I thank you for it."

"I don't know if I follow you, Father."

"In the trade, we call Notre Dame 'a little slice of heaven.' Well, it's time for me to get back to earth. To show I can fight, just like Rudy Ruettiger can fight. I'm going to the Philippines to do missionary work. Who knows? Even at my advanced age I might learn something new about myself. I like to think it's never too late."

He stood behind his desk and shook Rudy's hand warmly. "Look after this place when I'm gone, all right?"

Rudy nodded, fighting back tears.

"And send me a team picture," said the priest. "With you in it."

"That's a promise," said Rudy. He took a step forward and he and Father Cavanaugh embraced.

* * *

Fortune was painting a goalpost when Rudy walked up to him and stuck out his hand, holding the key to the maintenance shed.

"Thanks for everything, Fortune," he said.

Fortune scowled at the key. "What's this?" he said gruffly.

"The key to maintenance," said Rudy.

"Don't know nothing about it," said Fortune.

He went back to painting as Rudy, grinning, slipped the key into the older man's jacket.

"Hey, Fortune."

"Yeah?"

"I want you to promise if I dress for a game, you'll come and see me."

Fortune continued to paint in silence, but Rudy, knowing his friend's ways, waited patiently. Finally Fortune looked up and said, "Kid . . ."

"Yeah?"

"I don't like the damn sport."

"I know that."

"But you ever dress, I'll be there. No one's gonna keep Fortune away."

15

Dear Pop,

Well, I got what I wanted. I'm on the team, but boy oh boy, it's rougher than I thought. The workouts are all about how much pain you can take and still come back for more. Then I have to go back to my room, treat my wounds, and try to concentrate on the books. I can't afford to fall behind in my grades or it's good-bye to football, good-bye to Notre Dame. I'm lucky to have a friend like D-Bob, I've told you about him, he's some character. He helps me when I get overwhelmed. I don't want you to think I'm complaining—well, I guess I am because being a walk-on is kind of like lower than barnacles on the feeding chain, but at least I'm part of the team, and who knows? I keep at it and I'll dress for a game one day and be out there on the field. I always said I would, didn't I? Don't count me out.

But they do play some mean games out there in practice. One day I was getting in on the quarterback, really breathing on the guy, and the first team didn't like my aggression, like some upstart prep-team bozo is supposed to lay back and let you run all over him. They were out to kick my butt big-time. Well, they finally worked out a plan that the tackle would trap me and get me from behind. He took me down so hard and totally by surprise, I mean he blindsided me like some gangster getting you in an alley and I blacked out.

But don't get me wrong. I love this school, I love this team, although I'm not looking at it through rose-colored glasses anymore. Here at Notre Dame, football is a religion, it's a way of life to the coaches, the fans, the alumni. Winning is really important around here, but so is excellence. They really stress excellence of performance. Sometimes I wonder how I can possibly measure up to the high standards the coaches set for everybody. I walk into the locker room, and when I see myself in the mirror, I see this little guy. I never thought of myself as little before, I guess I thought of myself as big and mean, but when I look at these Notre Dame guys dressing beside me, when I see them in the mirror, I'm thinking, "Wait a minute, who is this little guy and what's he doing here with the grown-ups?" Meaning me.

I sometimes feel the football program pays more attention to the scholarship players, the hotshots, and us walk-ons are kind of an afterthought till we earn our stripes. Well, I'm going to earn mine, Pop, you can bet the house on that. I didn't come all this way to just lay down now and give up. My mind-set remains strong and basically positive, even with all this bitching I'm handing out, and I even help other prep-team guys deal with this process.

My goal remains what it's always been, to dress for a game. Right now I still seem to be invisible to Coach

Parseghian and the rest of his staff, but I'll go out there each day and bust my butt till they have to carry me off the field on a stretcher, and in the end I'll dress for a game. If it isn't this year, it'll be next year, but it's going to happen. There's no way they can stop me. It's like my determination is my religion. And when I walk down that tunnel and out onto the field, you're going to be there to see me, Pop. You and Ma and Frank and Johnny.

The rain had turned to sleet and was falling steadily from an iron-gray sky; the air was blue-knuckle cold. The prep team was getting the first team ready for Purdue, and the intensity was running high. Again and again Rudy got knocked to the ground, but no matter how severe the hit, in an instant he was back on his feet preparing for the next play. He had already earned himself a nickname— "Pinball Rudy"—and that pleased him, because having a nickname meant that he was beginning to be noticed, that he was beginning to make an impression. He even sensed that Parseghian himself was becoming aware of how much of himself he put into each sequence.

A play action pass developed. The quarterback took the handoff and faked a flip to a running back; the back jammed himself into the line. The quarterback, hiding the ball behind his hip, dropped back into the pocket, the tight end taking off downfield. As the prep-team safety tried to tackle the end who had broken free, Steve Mateus, the burly guard, came flying through the prep defense and, with the full force of his two hundred sixty-five pounds, leveled Rudy in a direct and brutal hit. For the first time, including all the thousands of hits he'd taken since spring, Rudy didn't get up. He lay on the ground motionless. Mateus stood over him, looking worried, and Coach Yonto came running up.

"Hey, Ruettiger, you all right, man?" said Mateus. "You with us, Pinball?"

Rudy started to stir. Mateus lifted him to his feet with one hand. Rudy was wobbly on his feet but managed a grin.

"Didn't feel a thing, Steve," he said. "Guess you're losing your touch."

Parseghian blew a whistle. "Sloppy execution," he shouted. "O'Hare, you got to do better on the deception. My grandmother would've known you're going to pass. Come on now, run it again and let's see a little magic."

Coach Yonto motioned Rudy out, but he shook his head vigorously. The play was run again, and this time when Mateus approached Rudy, in a position once again to take him down, he hesitated and pushed him away with his hands.

Rudy ran after him and yelled, "Hey, what the hell you doing?" He tugged at the lineman's jersey.

Mateus turned around and gaped at him, a shocked look on his face. No one talked to the big man that way; no one grabbed his jersey to make a point.

"Don't treat me like your kid brother," Rudy said angrily. "I'm playing defensive end for Purdue, remember? We've both got our assignments."

Mateus, O'Hare, and the other players were surprised by Rudy's outburst—all except for Roland Steele, who burst out laughing. Coach Yonto walked over.

"He's right, Mateus," said Yonto. "We don't need no Florence Nightingales out here. The idea is to get game tough. Save your compassion for church on Sunday."

Mateus gave Rudy a hard look and ran back to the

huddle. Coach Yonto slapped Rudy on the back, turned, and nodded to Parseghian, who nodded back. On the next play, a halfback sweep, Mateus sent Rudy flying through the air, and this time he didn't bother to help him up; in fact he didn't even glance at Rudy lying on the ground.

After standing under a hot shower until he felt that his body once again belonged to him, Rudy slowly dressed and left the locker room with Jim Obsetnick. Bent over and holding his ribs, he shuffled along like an eighty-year-old man. Mateus, Steele, and O'Hare came down from the main locker room, walking in the same direction.

Mateus caught up with Rudy and laid a heavy hand on his shoulder. Rudy winced. "Hey, little buddy, sorry about that. But Yonto got on my case."

"Don't be sorry. It's part of the game. You were just doing your job."

"Yeah, right," said Mateus. "But if you don't cool it out there, you're gonna get yourself killed."

"Wrong," said Rudy. "If I cool it out there I won't be helping you guys get ready for Saturday's game. That's *my* job. I'm just doing what I gotta do." He poked a finger into Mateus's chest and stared up at the giant lineman. "Got it?"

Mateus frowned at Rudy, then he started to laugh. He put his hands to his face, feigning fear. "Got it, Pinball."

Steele laughed, too, and said to Mateus, "When Rudy learns to stutter-step, you'll never lay a hand on him."

Jamie O'Hare looked disgusted. "Showboating," he said with a cold look at Rudy. "That's what he's all about. Coach's pet. He'll kill himself to please old Yonto."

"Hey, man, you're off base," Steele said to O'Hare.

"He's doing his job. Just do yours, okay? Coach was right. You ain't always concentrating out there."

"Yeah," said Mateus with a grin, nudging Steele. "Jamie's too busy checking out the chicks."

The three players lived in Pangborn Hall and they peeled off in that direction.

"Take 'er easy, Rudy," said Mateus.

"Yeah. See you tomorrow."

"Get some rest," said Mateus with a big grin. "I'll be comin' at you tomorrow."

"You'll have to catch me," said Rudy.

Obsetnick turned to Rudy as they continued on toward the seminary. "I can't believe it," he said.

"Can't believe what?" said Rudy. He was moving gingerly, aware of each painful step he took.

"I can't believe those guys even talked to you. In three years they've never said a word to me."

"Well, I'm always in their way," said Rudy. "I'm in their face. I guess they can't ignore me."

Rudy was deeply submerged in note taking when a buzzer signaled the end of class. He continued writing (history was not one of his easier courses, but then none of them were) as the students began to file out, then suddenly he was aware of a pair of legs standing next to him. He looked up the legs (shapely) to the white sweater, then on to the face. When he saw it was Mary McDonough, looking more beautiful than ever (if that was possible), he felt an ache in his groin, similar to the sensation of riding in a rapidly descending elevator. He hadn't seen her since spring.

"They allow Holy Cross students in this class?" she said.

He smiled at her and said, "You look great."

"You're evading the issue."

"What issue?" he said innocently. "I don't understand."

"You just never give up pretending, do you, Rudy?"

"You're way over my head," he said, smiling more broadly.

"I don't have time for this," she said, and started to walk away.

"Wait a second," he said.

She hesitated as he gathered his books and got up from his desk, grimacing with pain. "I've got two things to say to you, Mary. Are you listening?"

She glanced at her watch. "I'm late for my next class."

"I am now a student at Notre Dame. That's number one. Number two, I'm on the football team." He moved closer to her. "And I did it by the rules. I earned it. My grades at Holy Cross were excellent and I managed to get a transfer. I made the team as a walk-on because I'm willing to let myself get killed." He smiled ruefully as he rubbed his right knee. "And I'm afraid I'm well on my way."

Mary looked bewildered, then with a toss of her hair she said, "That's three," she said.

"Three what?"

"You said you had two things to say. But you just said three. Transfer, football, rules. That's three."

Rudy shook his head. "I just can't win with you, can I?"

"Well," she said, "congratulations on thing one. And thing three most of all. Rules *are* important. But as for thing two, I just can't bring myself to believe you. Got to go. See you later." She started to walk away.

"If you don't believe me," he said to her back, "come to practice."

She turned around and grinned at him, and Rudy felt that to be on the receiving end of a grin like that, so sweet and yet so mischievous, it would be difficult not to forgive her anything. "You know," she said, "I just might do that. I think I'll take you up on that little dare."

Again she turned to leave and Rudy said, "Hey, Mary?"

"Yes?"

"Nice seeing you again," he said.

She stared at him and then said softly, "I think it's nice seeing you, too, Rudy."

"You think?"

"If you're telling me the truth, it is."

The fall of 1974 was the busiest period of Rudy's life. Each morning he was up early to serve the novices breakfast in the seminary dining room. Then there were classes to attend, assignments to complete, football practice, and the homework again into the late hours of the evening. The schedule was a rough one, but Rudy had no complaints. For years he had dreamed of being a student at Notre Dame and a member of the football team, and now he had both, and if the reality was not quite so rosy as the dream, it didn't matter. He was living the life he had planned for himself and he couldn't imagine living any other. This was, as he'd come to think of it, his blue-and-gold dream come true, and all the hard classroom work and the brutal battering he took in practice was a small price to pay.

Two days after he ran into Mary McDonough, Rudy was emerging from a pile of bodies in practice when he spotted her standing with a notebook watching the action. She gave him a little wave and a smile. He ran over to the sidelines, removed his helmet to wipe sweat from his forehead, and casually reached out to touch the sleeve of her suede jacket. "Well?" he said.

"I'm embarrassed, Rudy. I've never been more embarrassed. Please forgive me."

"No problem."

"I just couldn't believe you're on the team."

"A shrimp like me, right?"

She still looked flustered and she was blushing. "I just feel like such a fool. . . ."

"Ruettiger, get your ass back here on the double," Coach Yonto yelled.

"Excuse me," said Rudy, replacing his helmet and buckling it under his chin. "You can see I'm needed on the field."

Mary watched him, at a loss for words.

In the tape room the next day, the trainer went through the complicated process of taping Rudy's body: cuts, abrasions, and bruises were everywhere. When the trainer was finished with him, he tapped his shoulder. "Thanks, Jeff," said Rudy, hopping down from the trainer's table. "I feel exactly like a mummy now."

Rudy was one of the few walk-ons who didn't have to tape himself and that was a recent concession to his work ethic; one day Jeff had simply taped Rudy's swollen thigh as though he was a member of the first team, and from then on he was a regular on the trainer's table. Rudy suspected that Coach Yonto had something to do with the special treatment. After all, Rudy got banged up more than any two other walk-ons; maybe the coaching staff was beginning to view him as a valuable property.

He hobbled over to his locker and, like an old man, groaned and sighed as he put on his uniform. Jim Obsetnick, sitting at the locker next to his, was staring off into space.

"Come on, Jim," said Rudy. "You're gonna be late again. You'll get a major ass chewing from Yonto. Nothing pisses the man off more than lateness."

Obsetnick looked up. "You know something, Ruettiger? Your John Wayne bullshit out there is beginning to grate on me. It makes us all look bad. Why don't you dial it down a notch? I mean what the hell are you trying to prove anyway?"

"Dial it down? I don't get what you mean."

Obsetnick stared at his unlaced shoes. "We're all getting sick and tired of hearing 'Why can't you put out like Ruettiger?' It's getting to be a big pain in the ass."

Rudy grabbed his helmet and stared at his friend. "I only know how to play one way. Hard."

"Come on, clue me in," said Obsetnick. "What do you get out of getting your butt kicked every day?"

"It's a job, Jim," said Rudy. "I'm doing my damn job, period."

"Believe me, this is a total waste of your time," said Obsetnick. "You're killing yourself, and for what? You have to be in at least one play during a regular-season game or you'll never go down on the books as officially being a part of the team. What are the chances of that happening to you and me? Zilch, zero, zip. Count on it, buddy—the only uniform you'll ever put on is that grungy thing you're wearing now."

"Jim, I'm going to get in a game."

Obsetnick shook his head. "You're kidding yourself, man. You're blowing some kind of weird smoke."

"If you hate it so much, you should quit," said Rudy. "You're not doing yourself or anybody else any good."

Obsetnick slowly laced a shoe. Without looking up he said, "I can't."

"Why not?"

"I've told you—family pressure. If I quit, my family won't pay my tuition."

"You mean that's the only reason you're here wearing this uniform?" said Rudy.

Obsetnick pulled on his pads. He paused and took a deep breath. "No, it's not the only reason, if you want to know the truth," he said softly. "I guess in a way I'm like you, Rudy, but I hate to admit it, even to myself. I still have the hope—part of me still suffers from the delusion I might get a chance to run out of that tunnel one day."

Rudy nodded and punched his friend on the shoulder. "Yeah, man, I know what you mean. It's some dream, ain't it?"

"Yeah," said Obsetnick, "it's some dream all right. I just can't figure out if it's a good dream or a bad dream."

The following morning Rudy was serving stacks of pancakes to the novices when he noticed Mary Mc-Donough standing in the doorway to the mess hall observing him. He motioned to her to wait a minute and got another student to relieve him. As he walked up to her he tried to appear casual, not overly eager to see her. It wasn't easy.

"What brings you over here?" he said.

"I've been thinking," she said. "You're really a pretty unusual guy. I want to write a story about you."

"You do? Are you kidding?"

"How many people have been through what you've been through, all the obstacles and everything? Guys like you just don't come to Notre Dame. You're really interesting, Rudy, and I believe people would like to read about you. You could be an inspiration for many readers."

"You're gonna make me blush," he said, grinning.

"I'm serious," she said.

"I can't see a story about me."

"You can't?"

"I'm a poor kid working his way through college. And I'm no star. I'm just a little guy who fought and begged his way on the team as a walk-on. And I'm no genius, either. I sweat bullets to get passing grades." He spread his arms. "I guess you could call me Mr. Everyman."

"But that's just the point, Rudy. Mr. Everyman had a dream of going to this elite school and the cards were stacked against him. But he didn't give up. He refused to settle for less than his dream. Don't you see? Don't you see what a terrific story that is?"

Rudy was silent for a moment, thinking. Then: "Tell you what," he said. "When I get to dress for a game, that's when you can write your story. A deal?"

"Okay," she said. "A deal."

"And Mary . . ." He hesitated.

"Yes?"

"You think I'm an interesting enough guy to have dinner with?"

Mary studied his face, then smiled. "Why not?" she said.

* * *

Rudy borrowed Fortune's van and drove to Joliet that Sunday to see the family. He hadn't been home since the summer and it bothered him that he had never received an answer to the long letter he'd written Danilo, although he knew he'd never be able to bring that up. There were a lot of things you couldn't say in the Ruettiger household, and suggesting that Danilo should have done something he neglected to do was definitely high on the list of forbidden topics.

It was a bleak fall day when he pulled up to the house. Johnny, Frank, and Danilo were hard at work building a patio addition at the rear of the house. It seemed to Rudy that they weren't overly excited to see him—even Johnny—and that bothered him, too. He paced back and forth in an agitated fashion as they continued to work.

It was Frank, as always, who started it. He looked up at Rudy and, with a sly grin, said, "We've been wondering around here. We wonder if you let your dreams run away with you. Like maybe you want something so bad you begin to believe it's true—you know what I mean? Like when it ain't there?"

"What you seem to be saying is, you don't think I'm on the team. Is that what you're saying, Frank?"

His older brother shrugged.

"You think I'm lying to you. Is that it?"

Danilo looked up. "Nobody said nothing about lying. But it's like we never see you or nothin'. You ain't on the bench. You ain't in any games."

"I've explained the whole thing to you, Pop. They can only dress sixty of ninety-five players. I'm not one of those sixty. Not yet. I'm in a supporting role right now."

"I believe you, Rudy," Johnny said.

"Supporting role," said Frank. "What's that supposed to mean? You hang around practice, is that it? You're there so much you begin to think you're on the team?"

"I guess I should get somebody to take pictures of me at practice," said Rudy, trying to keep control of his emotions. "Maybe that'll satisfy you." He pulled his sweater up to show his forearms covered with cuts and bruises. He pushed them in Frank's face. "Where do you suppose I got these? Professional wrestling? Dipping them in a meat grinder?"

"Okay, okay. You're like a kind of glorified water boy or something."

"You don't get banged up carrying water, Frank. You just don't get it, do you? We prep the first team each week. Like they're gonna play Navy? We run the Navy plays. Get it? Is that too complicated for you? Want me to draw a fucking diagram?"

"Hey," Danilo said.

His voice rising, Frank said, "If you're part of the team, my opinion of Notre Dame football just dropped to the pits."

"There is no *if*," said Rudy. "I wear a uniform. I block. I get the shit kicked out of me by guys like Steve Mateus. *I'm on the team, Frank.*"

"No need to shout," shouted Danilo.

"Leave him alone, Frank," said Johnny.

"Yeah," said Danilo, frowning at Frank. "Why you always gotta start up?"

"Tell him to leave *us* alone," said Frank, "coming here with all his bullshit."

"I guess it don't really matter," said Danilo, glancing at Rudy. "You're in the best university in the land. You're making good grades."

"But I'm also on the team, Pop. Read my lips. I am a member of the Notre Dame football team."

Danilo and Frank kept working on the fence. They didn't answer.

Rudy said to Johnny, "What's with them?"

"Search me, Rudy. Same old stuff goin' on." He shrugged.

Frank dropped his hammer on the ground and turned to Rudy. "It's simple," he said. "Every Saturday when we turn on the TV to watch the Irish, we see many, many players in the gold and blue. We don't see you."

"Either you're stupid or you're evil," Rudy said, his voice shaking with anger. "And all I can say is—screw you, brother. You'll all see me out on that field one day." Blind with rage, he picked up a barrel and heaved it against the fence with all his strength. "You will, I promise you that. You will. . . ."

16

On a grim and muddy afternoon in the late fall, the players' breath steaming out from their helmets, a scrimmage headed into high gear. The team was preparing for Saturday's game against USC, the final game of the regular season. The Irish hoped to end the season 11–1, their record marred only by the early-season loss to Purdue. The practice was as intense as any held all season; the coaches and players were beginning to show the effects of a long season. Even the calmest players were suffering from frayed nerves, and the obscenities were loud, the hits extra punishing.

"All right," Parseghian yelled, "third team and preps, let's go."

Jamie O'Hare broke with his group from the huddle. Rudy lined up at his usual position of defensive end. The quarterback called the signals, took the snap, and pitched it to O'Hare, who flared right, setting up for a halfback pass. The offensive end stepped out to block Rudy, but he froze when Rudy made a neat feint to his right, then quickly reversed to his left and went charging by the end. With a clear shot at O'Hare, Rudy dove into the quarterback, tackling him hard and clean and driving him to the ground. O'Hare rolled over, cursing, jumped to his feet, and charged Rudy. "Asshole," he screamed, and threw the football into Rudy's face.

"Pussy," Rudy screamed back, and jumped onto O'Hare, fists flying. The two rolled around on the muddy ground, wrestling and punching each other. Steve Mateus ran over to break them up, but Steele grabbed his jersey and held him back. "Ain't your dance, Steve," he said, grinning. The other players held back, too, but then Coach Yonto stepped up and dragged Rudy off O'Hare's chest.

"Brown nose," O'Hare yelled at Rudy. "Suck-ass. We'll continue this later."

"Anytime," said Rudy.

That brought Parseghian over. His face was red with anger as he dragged O'Hare to his feet.

"What's your problem, O'Hare?" he said. "Don't like physical contact? Would you prefer a noncontact sport? Ever think of taking up golf?"

"It's the last practice of the season, Coach," O'Hare whined, "and this idiot thinks it's the Super Bowl."

Parseghian glared at the player. "And you don't think it is the Super Bowl, right?"

O'Hare looked suddenly uncertain.

"You don't think it's important to prepare properly for USC. Is that what I'm getting from you?"

"Well, sure, Coach, of course. But—"

"No, you don't, O'Hare. The sad truth is, you don't think it's all that important. You've just summed up your entire sorry career here, crying like a baby when you take a hit." Parseghian got right in O'Hare's face, their chins nearly touching, and said, "If you had one tenth of Ruettiger's heart, you might be an All-American. As it is, you're spending the rest of this practice on the prep team. Being Ruettiger's teammate, maybe you'll learn something from him."

"But, Coach—"

"You heard me, O'Hare. Now move it."

Rudy smiled to himself as he limped back to his position. Mateus slapped him on the shoulder pads, as did a couple of the other players. Roland Steele caught his eye and gave him a broad wink.

After practice Rudy stood by Fran Martin's desk waiting to see Coach Parseghian.

"Remember when I broke in to see Coach?" he asked her, grinning. "Two years ago?"

"How could I possibly forget?" she said. "I thought you were about the craziest young man on campus."

"Shows you're a great judge of character," said Rudy. "I was crazy. I still am."

"That's not what I hear," said Fran. "Coach says you're an inspiration to the others."

"He said that?"

"Yep. And a compliment from Coach is something to treasure, believe me. He doesn't toss them around freely."

"Wow," said Rudy. "I'm really honored."

"You can see him now," she said. "He's off the phone."

Rudy walked in. "Coach," he said.

"Yes, Rudy. Nice job out there on O'Hare. I hope you gave him a wake-up call—he could use it. What can I do for you?"

"This won't take long," said Rudy. "First, I want to thank you for the chance to be part of the team this year."

"Rudy, I never thought I'd say this, but it's been a pleasure. Coach Yonto talked you up and it was a smart move on his part. Now, what can I do for you?"

"Well, this is kind of tough to say, Coach. But one of the many things I've learned this season is, no matter how hard I try, I'm never going to get above the prep team. I'm just not talented enough. I've kind of accepted that God made certain people to be football players and I'm not one of them."

Parseghian said, "I wish God would put your heart in some of my players' bodies."

"The thing is," said Rudy, "my father loves Notre Dame football. He loves it more than just about anything else in the world. He's on top of the world when they win, he dies a little when they lose. I've always been just like him that way. He doesn't think I'm on the team, Coach, because he doesn't see me on the sidelines." Rudy paused, then plunged ahead, saying, "Next year, my senior year, I want to be able to give him this gift. I would really appreciate it if you could . . . if you could let me dress for one game."

Parseghian shook his head and leaned back in his chair. "The NCAA really hamstrings us with this sixty-player rule. In certain positions we'll only have a single backup, and you know every year we compete for the national championship."

Rudy's face fell. Parseghian studied him and then continued in a softer, more confidential tone. "Rudy, is this just for your father? Is there more to it than that?"

"I guess there is more," said Rudy, looking up, his mouth twisting with emotion. "I guess it's my answer to everybody who ever said, 'You're a shrimp. You can't do this, you can't do that. How can a guy like you play Notre Dame football? You got no ability, you got no size.' That's all I ever heard from my older brother, from guys in my high school, from guys I worked with in the mill. They go by what they see, not what's inside me. And the thing is, nobody sees me in practice, so it's like it almost doesn't count. If I'm not on the field, I'm not on the team. It's that simple."

As he drummed his fingers on his desk Coach Parseghian studied Rudy. "Okay," he said at last.

"Okay? Did you say okay?" Rudy's voice was rising with excitement.

"You deserve it," said Parseghian. "You'll dress for one game next season."

"Oh God, Coach, I can't tell you what this means to me." He stuck out his hand. "Can we shake hands on it?"

"Of course we can," said Parseghian, standing. "I would consider it a pleasure."

That night, from a phone booth at Corby's, Rudy called Danilo and told him Coach Parseghian had promised to dress him for a game next season.

"Hey, that's great," said Danilo. "That's just great, Rudy."

"You proud of me, Pop?"

There was the slightest pause before Danilo said, "Yeah, son, you know that. I'm proud of all my kids. You don't have to ask. So you know what game yet?"

Rudy laughed. "Gotta get a schedule first," he said. "I'll probably know a couple days before. You'll come, won't you?"

"It's next year," said Danilo. "That's a long ways off."

"Yeah, I know, but you'll come, right?"

"Damn right," said Danilo. "Just try and keep me away."

Rudy beamed. "I'll have seats for you and Ma, Johnny, and Frank."

"You better."

"Well, Pop, I gotta go. I'm runnin' up the bill."

After a long pause Danilo said, "I guess I've been a doubter, but you're provin' me wrong. You can do anything you set your mind to. Yeah—you know, words don't come easy to me. But I am proud of you."

He hung up and Rudy, smiling, returned to the table to join Mary. "So when do you want the story to come out?" he said.

"The day before your dress game."

"Okay. What do you want to know about me?"

"Everything. School, sports, your brothers, your parents, your girlfriends, your fears, your dreams. Everything."

"That's a tall order," he said.

"I won't use anything you don't want me to use."

"I haven't had exactly a glamorous life, Mary."

"Interesting's better than glamorous," she said. "And I know yours has been interesting."

"I'm glad you think so. You spend a day in the mill, you might change your mind."

Pen poised and notebook open, Mary said, "Come on, Rudy, don't be shy. Start talking. I want everything."

He looked into her eyes, smiling, and said, "So do I, Mary. So do I."

Two days later Rudy picked up the *South Bend Tribune* and was shocked at the headline: COACH PARSEGHIAN RETIRES. He sped through the article, picking up the highlights. Apparently, Parseghian's decision had been made early in the fall, immediately following the Navy game, but he had informed only the university higher-ups. He cited important family considerations and constant pressure; the fun, he said, had gone out of football. The article went on to extol Parseghian's many virtues: *Coach Parseghian,* the article stated, *set a new standard of excellence for both Notre Dame and college football. We all must be thankful that Ara Parseghian led the team's fortunes for eleven victorious seasons. His record—95-17-4 (.836)—is nearly the equal of Frank Leahy's .855. We will miss you, Ara. Good luck!*

Rudy met D-Bob at the student center at noon. D-Bob, with a big grin, came bounding up to Rudy, who sat on the steps gloomily studying the paper, still finding it difficult to accept the news.

"Victory, victory, that's our cry," sang D-Bob. "V-I-C-T-O-R-Y spells victory! I got in, Gipper. I

fooled 'em down at ol' Miami Law School and they
done tendered an invitation to yours truly.''

Rudy stood, smiled, and hugged his friend. "Great,
just great, D-Bob. I'm really happy for you. It's what
you wanted, right?''

"Well, it ain't Harvard, but it'll do." He studied
Rudy's face. "I detect some strain around your eyes
and mouth, old friend. What's buggin' you?''

Rudy shoved the newspaper into D-Bob's hands
and he read the story quickly. "Well, I'll be god-
damned," he said. "Who's this Dan Devine, the new
coach? Is he any good?''

"From the Green Bay Packers," said Rudy unen-
thusiastically. "He's supposed to be terrific." He took
the paper back from D-Bob, folded it neatly, and stuck
it in his hip pocket. "You know I saw Coach Parseghian recently and he promised to let me dress for a
game. I did tell you, didn't I?''

"About a hundred times is all.''

"Well, he must have known he was leaving.''

"Look," said D-Bob, "he'll work it out for you.
I'll bet he'll talk to Devine.''

"I'm sure he's got bigger things on his mind than
me.''

D-Bob slung an arm around Rudy's shoulder.
"Life's sure curious, ain't it, buddy? I'm the bearer of
good tidings just as you come along bearing rotten
ones. Just go figure.''

"I worked all year to get Coach's respect," said
Rudy. "I beat myself to a pulp. And I got it, too. Now
it means starting all over again with a new coach.
Having to prove myself all over again." He sighed.

"Shit!" He forced a laugh. "Nobody said it would be easy, right?"

"You're right about that, Gipper. But I tell you, you're gonna dress for a game and I'll be back here to watch you when you do. Depend on it."

Rudy said, "I'll have a ticket waiting for you."

"Come with me," said D-Bob. "I have to meet someone." As they walked toward the Huddle a number of students greeted Rudy, and D-Bob grinned and nudged him. "You're becoming a famous guy. I guess I should count myself lucky to be your bosom buddy."

"I don't know about the bosom part," said Rudy.

"You should run for a student office next year."

"Lay off, D-Bob. When do you leave for Miami?"

"Not sure. To paraphrase the immortal Dick Nixon, our late and unlamented, you'll still have me to kick around for a while." He punched Rudy on the arm. "We've had a helluva goddamn run, haven't we, Gipper?"

"Yeah, we've done pretty good," said Rudy.

"I'm serious about flying up. When you dress for a game, I'll be here."

Rudy kicked a pebble along as they walked—a habit from his boyhood—his expression pensive, melancholy. "There's no way I can thank you for all you've done. Without you I wouldn't be here now."

D-Bob got Rudy's head in a vise and squeezed. "Stop with the bullshit already," he said. "You want to see a grown man cry?"

Rudy smiled. "Spare me."

They swung around to the Huddle and Rudy was surprised to see D-Bob greet Elsa Schmidt, the girl he'd tried to interest him in two years earlier. Rudy had to admit she no longer looked so plain. And her smile, as she greeted D-Bob, was warm and radiant.

"I'm sure you remember Elsa," said D-Bob with a wink. "I met her thanks to you, pal. And a few weeks ago we met again. She's my girl now and she's coming with me to Miami. Isn't that goddamn something?" he said, pounding Rudy on the back.

"Dennis," she said disapprovingly.

D-Bob laughed. "Oh, oh, I forgot. Not allowed to swear anymore. It reveals moral decadence and a paucity of vocabulary. But what's a poor lapsed Catholic to do?" He put his arms around Elsa and kissed her. "So what do you think, Gipper?"

"I think I did you a bigger favor than I ever realized," said Rudy.

"You know something?" said D-Bob. "When you're right, you're right. And for once, Gipper, that's exactly what you are."

Dear Johnny,

Well, we had a good season, I mean how can you knock a 10–2 record? But it's hard to defend a national crown, and '73 was just one terrific team. Maybe our standards around here are just too high, but everyone expects a winner at Notre Dame, a championship team every year, and anything else just won't cut it. But that just can't happen.

Anyway, Dan Devine has been handed a fine team by Coach Parseghian, and as far as me getting in a game, I keep telling myself Notre Dame means so much more than just getting in a game. Only eleven guys can be on the field at once. What about the other eighty or so that never get to play in every game and some in no games at all? Do they just sit around and mope? No, we're in the game, our hearts and heads, even if our butts are on our helmets on the sidelines, or in the stands if you're a walk-on like me. But we're all part of the team, we're members of the blue and gold. And we're proud, Johnny. Plus we're getting a good education, one of the best around.

Johnny, I wish you were here. You're the only one back there that has any true belief in me. Every time the team scores, I look up at Touchdown Jesus and I think of you and Frank and Pop watching on TV and I feel something's missing.

I just want you to know I haven't given up on my dream, not by a long shot. I'll keep on bangin' heads, keep strong and resolute, and prove myself to Devine like I did to Parseghian—I'm learning some big words here thanks to my buddy D-Bob—and one fine day I'm gonna be out there on the field. I know you believe me and I know you'll be proud of me. I hope the same is true of Frank and Pop.

Love, Rudy

PART

FIVE

☆

1975

17

He joked with Fran Martin and then walked into the office that was once Ara Parseghian's. Dan Devine, the new Notre Dame coach, a wiry, bespectacled man in his forties, was absorbed in a number of charts spread out on his desk until Rudy cleared his throat. When Devine looked up, his expression was mildly irritated.

"Yes," he said. "What is it?"

Rudy stuck out his hand and said, "Rudy Ruettiger." He hoped for a sign of recognition ("Oh yeah, the kid who busted his butt last year. Coach Yonto speaks highly of you"—something like that), but there was none.

Devine's grip was cool and unresponsive. "What can I do for you?" he said, glancing pointedly at his charts.

"Well," said Rudy, "I was a walk-on last year and—"

"I don't believe in walk-ons," Devine cut in, "especially considering the caliber program we have here. I have quality athletes on scholarships and we'll probably play sixty of them at most. I've got to keep the others busy."

"I know that," said Rudy, "but can I say something?"

For the first time there was a hint of interest in the coach's eyes. Most kids would have taken the hint and left, but not this one. There was something different about him, something strongly focused and inwardly intense. Devine shoved back in his seat. "It seems to me you're saying it."

"I really believe the prep team is important," said Rudy. "We make a difference. We bust our chops. We get the first team ready, and you don't have to worry about us getting hurt. Not that we don't get hurt, but you don't have to worry about it." He grinned. "Around here we're known as cannon fodder."

Devine played with a pencil as he stared at Rudy. "My bottom thirty-five can prep," he said. "It'll toughen 'em up."

Rudy put his hands on the coach's desk and leaned forward. "Sir, if I could just show you, prove to you that we make a difference. Ask Coach Yonto. He knows what we can do."

"I've discussed this matter with Coach Yonto. We plan to do things differently this year." When Rudy, clearly stunned and hurt, didn't answer, Devine continued. "Look, Ruettiger, you don't know me, I don't know you. But I do know who you are."

Rudy looked at the coach, whose expression had softened. "You do?"

"Coach Yonto thinks well of you and he made a special plea to keep you on the team." Devine hesitated, then said, "You understand that football here at Notre Dame is a serious business. There's no room for sentiment when so much is at stake. But Coach Yonto really went to bat for you, Ruettiger. He seems to think you'll serve some kind of useful purpose. So . . . against my better judgment you're still on the team."

"I am?"

"You'd better live up to Coach Yonto's billing," said Devine. "I'll have my eye on you. You realize you're taking time away from one of my other players."

"You won't be sorry, Coach," said Rudy. "I can't tell you how good this makes me feel."

Devine gave him a brief nod in dismissal and then returned to his charts.

Rudy had learned a little about the new coach in the past few days. Notre Dame had wanted him as far back as 1964, and now that they had him, they were confident he was the one man who could fill Parseghian's shoes. After one practice, Rudy and the other players could see that like Parseghian, his personality was cool and assured, but that his operational methods were totally different. Whereas Parseghian had struck them as somewhat aloof and dictatorial, Devine was low-key and seemed to blend into the background, letting Yonto, Warren, and his other coaches deal directly with the players; he was much more willing to delegate authority than Parseghian had been.

Rudy was the spiritual leader of the prep team now. The others looked to him for guidance. When he wasn't in the middle of a play, he was clapping his hands, exhorting his teammates. Before the first game of the season, against Boston College, practice was going poorly and Yonto had lost his temper, screaming at the players over a series of sloppy plays. Coach Devine had needed to rebuild the offensive line, since five starters had graduated; most of the interior men were capable technicians, but only Mateus was a dominating player. There was great speed in the backfield—Roland Steele had developed into an All-American—but the team hadn't yet jelled and the practices were ragged: frenetic one moment, lethargic the next.

Roland Steele grabbed Rudy and took him aside. "Look, man, the prep team's playing like crap. They're dogging it. It's your job to keep them up."

Rudy nodded and ran over into the middle of a circle of players. They were all physical giants next to him, but they treated him with respect. He yelled at them, shook his fist in their face. "You guys stink," he said. "You're lying down. You're dead. You're playing like pussies. My grandmother could run through you and my grandmother is dead. Coach is ready to puke. Come on—show these shitheads you're men. Beat on 'em, waste 'em, blow 'em away! *Let's go!*"

They listened intently to this pint-sized bantam rooster, then they broke the circle screaming, fired up. On the next play the prep team intercepted a pass and returned it for a touchdown; Rudy sent a first-team guard flying with a crunching tackle. Across the field, Steele gave Rudy a thumbs-up as Yonto directed his wrath at the first team.

Rudy had not figured to dress for a game early in the schedule, but as each home game came and he consulted the dress list in the main locker room and his name wasn't posted, he grew more somber.

Notre Dame beat a tougher-than-expected Boston College 17–3.

They blanked Purdue 17–0.

The Irish faced an undefeated Northwestern team in their home opener and pounded them into submission, 31–7. Rudy was in the stands rooting them on.

They then lost to Michigan State, 10–3. Rudy felt sick as he watched their feeble offense that Saturday, but he rooted them on.

The next two games for the Irish—games everyone assumed would be breathers in preparation for a powerful Southern California team—turned into nightmares and near disasters.

They were forced to come from behind to beat North Carolina, who entered the game with an 0–5 record.

Then, down again with just thirteen minutes to play, they won a squeaker over the lowly Air Force, 31–30.

The weeks were passing; fall was turning toward winter. Each week Rudy checked the dress list, his heart in his throat, and each week the same old story: his name wasn't there. Finally, only one home game remained, Georgia Tech.

Following an afternoon practice, Coach Yonto pulled Rudy aside and said, "Listen, kid, I know how anxious you are to dress for this game."

"Anxious isn't the word for it, Coach. I'm dying inside. If I don't dress for Georgia Tech, my dreams are down the drain."

"Well, I can't promise you anything—you know I'm not in charge," said Yonto. "And things have been kind of rough around here lately."

Rudy nodded; Coach Yonto didn't have to spell it out. It was no secret that Devine was having a difficult first year at the helm. The team had already lost two games, barely survived two that everyone felt they should have won easily, and they had yet to face the Pitt Panthers and the phenomenal tailback Tony Dorsett, who was eating up yardage against everybody. Rumors of Devine's dismissal were making the rounds of the campus, especially after the team's horrendous showing against the Air Force team. Beating them by one point was like a bad loss. To make matters worse, Devine had turned down the Cotton Bowl invitation; no one was quite sure why and Devine was keeping his own counsel.

"I'm hoping you can dress for Georgia Tech," Yonto continued, "but I can't give you a positive yes. God knows, you deserve it, Rudy. You've given me everything I've ever asked of you. But Coach Devine makes these decisions, and he's got a lot on his mind."

After talking with Coach Yonto, he and Mary, who was now a regular at the practices, rushed to a phone so that Rudy could call home. It was five o'clock and Danilo had just gotten home from the mill.

"Pop," said Rudy, breathless with nervousness. "Don't make any plays for Saturday, okay?"

"Yeah? What's up?" said Danilo.

"I think I'm gonna be in against Georgia Tech."

"Oh yeah? Really?"

Rudy sensed his father's skepticism. The season

was nearly over, after all, and he hadn't gotten closer to the field than a good seat on the fifty-yard line. "Coach Yonto thinks my chances are good," he said.

Rudy hung up the phone, feeling strangely let down. Sensing his mood, Mary gave him a smile and blew him a kiss.

"I need to go somewhere right now," he said. "Will you come with me?"

"Where?"

"You'll see."

"Ah, we're being mysterious." But she fell into step beside him. Most of the trees on campus were leafless now, and that saddened Rudy, not because of the changing of seasons and the advent of winter, but because football 1975 was nearly over, his college career was nearly over, and his chance of dressing for a game had dwindled down to one remaining day. He tried not to look at the trees.

Mary broke the silence. "So Coach Yonto really came through?"

Rudy turned to her, looking worried. "Well, not exactly," he said. "It was more like 'You have a shot, Rudy, but it's up to Coach Devine.' The awful part is, my dad *still* doesn't believe I'm an official member of the team. Maybe he's right, you know. Maybe I've been kidding myself."

"Oh, come on, Rudy. You haven't gotten where you are with that kind of self-pity junk."

"Self-pity junk? Is that how it sounds?"

"That's what I'm hearing right now."

He looked at Mary and finally nodded. "I guess you're right. I feel like somebody stuck a knife in my heart and I'm struggling like hell to get it out."

"Keep struggling," she said with a grin. "You're at your best when you struggle."

"Remember what you promised me," he said. "If I don't dress, there's no article. That's the deal, right?"

"You know me," she said. "I play by the rules."

They came to the Grotto and Rudy said, "This is my last, best hope. D-Bob's always saying that—my last, best hope."

Mary shook her head. "I don't believe in this kind of stuff."

Rudy handed her a dollar. "Well, just on the off chance," he said. "Just do it for me. It can't hurt. Light a candle for me to get on that dress list tomorrow. . . . Please, Mary."

Mary shook her head again and handed Rudy his dollar back. "I can pay my own way," she said. She opened her purse. "Do you think putting in more will give you some kind of edge"—she rolled her eyes upward—"with Him?"

"I guess I'm superstitious enough to think so," he answered. "But I don't want you spending your money."

"You're my investment, Mr. Ruettiger," she said. "No Rudy in uniform, no story." She withdrew a ten-dollar bill, stuffed it in the box, lit ten candles, knelt, bowed her head for a moment, muttered something under her breath, then stood and turned to face Rudy.

"There's no way I can miss the dress list now," he said, smiling.

The next day, before practice, in full gear, Rudy stood outside the scholarship players' locker room. He took a deep breath and crossed himself. Then he entered. Steve Mateus and Roland Steele were the first players to spot him. Mateus refused to meet his gaze and Steele, with an edgy smile, said, "Hey, Rudy, my man," then he looked away. So without even looking at the list, he knew he wouldn't dress for the Georgia Tech game. But he had to see for himself, he had to take the direct hit. He walked over to the dress board, trying to appear casual. He looked down at it and his name wasn't there, and even though he knew it wouldn't be, he stood there frozen, a vise tightening on his chest, his eyes fastened on the list but seeing nothing. Soon tears welled up in his eyes; he couldn't help himself and was beyond caring who saw him.

Then he was aware that Mateus was saying something to him. "Sorry. . . ."

He ran out the door.

In the walk-on locker room Rudy ripped off his uniform as Jim Obsetnick, who was dressing, watched him in alarm.

"Hey, what's up, man?" he said. "I've never seen you so bent out of shape."

"I'm undressing," said Rudy. "I'm removing my uniform."

"But we got a practice coming up."

"Not me," said Rudy. "This is *it* as far as me and Notre Dame football go. To hell with Devine, to hell with the team—to hell with it all."

"Didn't make the dress list, huh?"

"I quit," said Rudy. "I'm outta here. No more playing the sucker for me."

"Come on," said Obsetnick, "don't go off the wall on me. In two years you've never missed a practice and the last one of your senior year you quit? Does that make any sense? What kind of shit is this?"

"I've had it," said Rudy. "I can quit if I want to. It's a free country and I quit. So leave it alone."

"Well," said Obsetnick, "what if I tell you I don't want you to?"

Rudy stopped undressing and turned to his friend. "What'd you say?"

"You heard me."

"What's it to you if I quit or not?"

Obsetnick stared at a knee pad, then strapped it on. "You're the reason I stayed on this year. The only reason."

Rudy glanced angrily at Obsetnick, then tossed his uniform in the locker and quickly began to dress. "Sorry, buddy," he said. "I've taken enough bullshit around here to last a lifetime, and now it's time I got myself a life. I've been cannon fodder too damn long. So have you. We're suckers and it's time to smarten up."

Obsetnick slowly shook his head. "You're so full of shit, man. All the things you said, all the things you stood for."

"Don't lecture me, Jim," said Rudy. "You're beginning to seriously piss me off." He pulled on his coat and started for the door.

"So you're just another asshole, after all," shouted Obsetnick, and threw his helmet at the door an instant after Rudy disappeared through it.

"I'm sorry, Pop. I'm sorry, Pop. I'm sorry, Pop. Things just didn't work out. I'm sorry." Rudy sat in the stands staring at the empty field, muttering to himself. He shivered as he dropped his head in his hands. A group of girls ran onto the field, stood in a circle, and sang the Alma Mater. Probably practicing for Saturday's game, Rudy thought, and not even their collective beauty and gaiety could lighten his heart.

He tried to resist the emotional pull of the song, but even in his present state he felt an actual chill; the words hit him hard as they always did. Was it possible to love a place and a tradition all your life and then throw it away in a single day? Maybe not, Rudy thought bitterly, but it was sure worth a try.

The sound of someone climbing the stairs aroused him from his dark thoughts. Fortune sat down next to him heavily, with a sigh. "Those steps get steeper every day. You noticed that? No, I don't guess you have, as young as you are."

Rudy smiled wanly but said nothing.

"What are you doing here? Don't you have practice?"

"Yeah, but you notice I'm not there," said Rudy. "And there won't be any practice for me tomorrow, either. Or the day after that."

"Oh, is that so?"

"I quit," said Rudy. "I'm finished with them."

"You quit," said Fortune, nodding, sucking his teeth. "Is this Rudy Ruettiger I'm talking to?"

"I'm fed up, Fortune. I can only take so much. They've used me and I've gotten zero in return."

"Since when are you the quitting kind?"

"I don't see the point anymore. I gave. I got nothing back. Maybe it's better to give than receive, but what the hell, if you don't *ever* receive, you begin to go crazy, you know?"

Fortune made a disgusted clicking sound with his tongue. "So you didn't make the dress list. Well, there are greater tragedies in life than that, in case you haven't heard."

"I wanted to be able to run out on the field for my dad," said Rudy, his voice beginning to tremble. "I'm twenty-four years old, not a kid anymore, and I haven't done anything with my life. I need to prove something to my dad—to a whole lot of people."

Fortune studied him carefully. "Prove what?"

"That I'm somebody. That I count." Rudy choked on the words and felt tears building behind his eyes.

Fortune rose slowly to his feet. He looked down at Rudy, and suddenly laughing, he said, "You are so full of crap, kid. You know that?"

"I'm not making any friends today," said Rudy, "that's for sure."

"Stand up," Fortune roared suddenly.

Startled by the vehemence in the older man's voice, he instinctively obeyed.

"Look at you," said Fortune. "You're five-feet-nothing and a hundred and nothing. You got hardly a speck of athletic ability, and what do you do? You hang in with the best college football team in the land for two years, is all. Plus you're also gonna walk out of here with a degree from the University of Notre Dame. That's all you've accomplished. Nothin' to speak of at all."

Fortune's eyes were ablaze and Rudy had to look away. "In this life," the older man continued, "you don't have to prove nothing to nobody . . . except yourself. And after what you've gone through, if you haven't done that by now, it ain't never gonna happen."

Rudy made no effort to hide the tears as he looked into his friend's eyes. "You're telling me I should stay with the team?"

Fortune nodded. "If they'll have you back. Do it for them if you can't do it for yourself. You stand for something around here, kid. I hear you talked about. You're the little guy with the heart of a big guy. I guess you could say you're an inspiration."

"You know the saddest thing," said Rudy. "I couldn't get you in here to see your first game."

"Hell," said the older man, "I've seen too many games in this stadium."

"What do you mean? I thought you'd never been to a game."

"I've never seen a game in the stands."

Rudy stared at him, amazed. "You were a player?"

"Yup." Fortune's grin was slow and warm. "Rode the bench for two years and thought I wasn't being played because of my color, got filled up with a lot of bad attitude, so I quit. And you know something, kid? Not a week goes by I don't regret it. And I guarantee, not a week's gonna go by in your life you won't regret walking out—letting 'them' get the best of you."

Rudy was listening with full attention now, his mouth open in awe.

"You hear me clear enough?" said Fortune. "Get your ass back to practice tomorrow and give 'em all the hell you got in you."

The next day, the teams were going through their normal drills. Steve Mateus got up from the ground, and as he was about to run back to the huddle, something caught his eye. Another player grabbed Roland Steele by the shoulders and pointed. Everyone on the field was suddenly frozen in place, watching as Rudy, back in uniform, walked toward them.

"Knew the idiot couldn't stay away," said Steele with a grin, and loud enough for Rudy to hear. "He digs punishment too much."

Mateus started clapping slowly and rhythmically and others gradually joined in until there was a loud percussion of clapping hands. Rudy stood with a foolish grin on his face as the clapping and shouting increased in volume. He plugged his fingers in his ears.

Coach Yonto walked up to Rudy and said brusquely, "Welcome back, Ruettiger. Did you have a nice vacation?"

Rudy touched his helmet in a mock salute. "Fabulous, Coach. I stayed in bed late and nobody beat up on me."

From the tower, Devine stuck his head out, bullhorn in hand. "What's going on down there, Coach? Let's get to work."

"Get your ass out there," Yonto told Rudy, "and wake this crew up. They're asleep on their feet."

After practice, Roland Steele whispered something to Steve Mateus, then huddled in the locker room with the other first-team players. He quickly dressed, slipped out of the locker room and hurried down the hall to Devine's office, winked at Fran Martin, and strolled into the coach's office with all the confidence of an All-American. Devine was busy with his ever-present charts.

"Coach, I got a problem," said Steele, leaning on Devine's desk.

"Well, Roland," said Devine with a brief smile, "that's what I'm here for. Maybe I can help."

"That's what I'm hoping, Coach."

"Just don't request any more tickets. It seems you bring half of South Bend in here. The half that likes to party."

"I'm blessed with a lot of friends," said Steele, "but that's not why I'm here." His expression was serious; determination tightened his mouth. Devine was comfortable with the laid-back Steele, who wore his fame lightly and always had a smile and joke for everyone. But this was a different Steele. He suddenly felt a pang of apprehension in his gut.

"Well, why are you here, Roland?" he said.

"I want Rudy Ruettiger to dress for Saturday's game. It's the last home game of the year and his last chance. You know he's a senior."

"There is no room for walk-ons," said Devine.

"He's busted his balls for two years," said Steele. "Nobody's worked harder. I mean *no*body."

"Sorry," said Devine. "I have other deserving players, some of them scholarship kids, who never dress. You know that."

"Well, Coach," said Steele slowly, "here's the way I see it. You can make room for Rudy or not make room. That's your call. But I've worked with him for two years, and I believe he's helped make us a better team. He's spilled a lot of blood doing it, too. He deserves a shot. So what I'm thinking is, he can dress in my place."

Devine stared at Steele and broke a pencil in half.

"Are you crazy?" he said. "I can't do that. It's ridiculous. Georgia Tech is the number-one offensive team in the country. You're an All-American, Roland, and our captain. Act like it."

Steele's easy smile—the trademark of the man—was nowhere in evidence. His stare was flat and cold, and Devine had trouble meeting it. "Sorry, Coach. I guess I feel strongly about this. . . ." He opened his bag, removed his jersey and laid it on Devine's desk, turned, and without another word walked out.

As Devine reached for the jersey, shaking his head in exasperation, there was a knock on the door and Steve Mateus walked in. His jersey was draped over his arm. He deposited it on top of Steele's.

"I want Ruettiger to dress in my place," he said. As Coach Devine started to speak the big lineman held up his hand. "There's nothing to talk about, Coach." He turned on his heel and walked out.

There was a third, a fourth, a fifth, a sixth knock on Devine's door. The players streamed in and deposited their jerseys on the coach's desk. The pile grew higher and higher. Devine sat behind his desk, speechless.

18

After practice on Friday morning, the day before the last home game of the year, Coach Yonto blew a whistle and said that Coach Devine had an announcement to make. A moment later Devine appeared. He walked directly over to Rudy, gave him a long look, then stared at the assembled players and said, "Yesterday I had one of the most unusual experiences of my life. Most of my starting defensive and offensive units visited me in my office, all with an identical request. They wanted to give this player—Ruettiger here—their place in the lineup for tomorrow's game. You ever heard anything to beat this? I know I sure haven't."

He looked at Rudy unsmilingly. "This struck me as more than unorthodox, more than a simple case of insubordination. Frankly, it struck me as downright crazy and negative in morale terms. But then I got to thinking about it. It occurred to me that if all of you cared this much, if you felt this strongly about Ruettiger dressing for a game, then what logic would allow me to impose a veto? I consulted Coach Yonto and he told me, not for the first time, that in all his years at Notre Dame, no player had been more committed to team excellence than Ruettiger here." He turned to Rudy and a hint of a smile crossed his face. "Report to the locker room and check with Dan. There's a game uniform ready for you."

"This is mine?" said Rudy.

"That it is," said Dan. "Haven't had a body it would fit in more than ten years. Scully, I forget his first name. Small guy, like you."

"My number's forty-five," said Rudy. "I like that. A nice sound to it." He ran his fingers over the number, then over the letters of his name.

"Sorry I had to stencil your name on the jersey," said Dan. "This just came up all of a sudden."

"It's okay, Dan. At least I won't be walkin' out there tomorrow with no name." Rudy picked up his uniform—the gold pants, the white-and-blue jersey, and finally the brilliantly gold helmet. "Am I dreaming?" he said with a broad grin, setting the helmet on his head. Perfect fit.

"I don't think so," said Dan.

"Well, if I am, don't wake me up."

Rudy and Mary strolled over to the student lounge. The weather had turned sharply colder and Rudy wore his ancient Notre Dame jacket—now practically in tatters—buttoned up to the neck. He was rarely without the jacket except in the heat of summer; wearing it was his way of keeping Peter Sturges close to him, alive. He dreaded the day when his jacket would be too worn to wear. But he would never throw it away; he would hang it in his closet—in a prominent spot where he would always see it—and keep it forever.

He called home and Frank answered the phone.

"Pop's out bowlin'," he said curtly. "You want Ma?"

"That's okay," said Rudy. "I'll talk to you."

"Sure," said Frank.

"It's for real this time," Rudy burst out, his voice cracking with excitement. "I'll be in uniform, on the sidelines. I may not get in the game—Georgia Tech's tough and they won't stick me in if the game's on the line. But I've got my uniform, I've already tried it on. And I've got my number—forty-five. And I've got tickets for the four of you."

Rudy could hear the hesitation in Frank's voice as he said, "You want me to come?"

"Yeah, Frank, I want you here."

"I don't know," Frank said. "Me and some guys had talked about driving up to Michigan for deer."

"Come on," said Rudy, "not this weekend. You can't do that. Look, I've never asked you for anything in my life—"

"Like hell," said Frank with a short laugh. "You were always beggin' your way into my pickup games. Remember?"

"Yeah, Frank. The thing is, I want you here. You and Pop and Ma and Johnny. This is my big deal."

After a pause Frank said, "Okay."

"Don't forget my number. Forty-five."

"I think I'll be able to spot you, bro. Just keep an eye out for the big guy."

Rudy hung up and turned to Mary. He took her hand. "The story's out?"

"This afternoon," she said. "I'll bring a copy to the pep rally."

"How did it turn out?"

"I made you a hero." She squeezed his hand and smiled. "It wasn't all that hard to do. Just a little fictionalizing here and there."

"I got to tell you something, Mary," he said, "something I've never admitted to anybody before. Even to myself, in a way. I've talked a lot about my dreams, what I planned to accomplish and all. People think I'm confident, even cocky maybe. You know— that short guy with a complex. But the truth is a whole lot different. I've wanted this—being here at Notre Dame, making the team—more than I've ever wanted anything in my life. But deep down inside I never thought it would happen, not in a thousand years. I can't tell you how many times I woke up in a cold sweat, knowing I was just a con job and was bound to fail. But I kept my fear of failure to myself—you could almost say *from* myself. If anything, my fear acted as a spur to make me try harder." He stared into her eyes. "Does what I'm saying surprise you?"

She shook her head. "Not at all. You're a pretty complex person, Rudy. Maybe one day I'll have to write a second story about you."

"Yeah," he said, grinning, "when the miniseries comes out."

* * *

Late that afternoon, Rudy walked over to the small basketball court beside St. Mary's Lake. He took a basketball from his gym bag and started playing a game of horse, shooting from different spots on the court. With his heavy class load and all the hours of practice, he didn't get over there much anymore, but over the past four years he'd stayed in touch with Garson Faulk, the young black kid he'd met on his first day in South Bend. They still played one-on-one games occasionally, but Garson, now nineteen, had sprouted up to six-feet-four and Rudy didn't stand a chance against him. Garson was a housepainter now, working with his father. Rudy kept nagging at him about continuing his education, and recently, at Rudy's suggestion, he had said he might get over to Holy Cross Junior College for an interview.

At five-thirty, as dusk was beginning to settle over the campus, Garson rode up on his bike. He jumped off, grabbed the ball out of Rudy's hands, and promptly swished a twenty-footer.

"Foul," said Rudy.

"Are you kidding?" said Garson, leering down at Rudy. "A clean steal."

Rudy reached into his pocket and withdrew a ticket. "For tomorrow," he said casually, handing it to Garson. "Not on the fifty-yard line, but close. You'll like the view."

Garson stared at the ticket and then at Rudy; he broke into a huge, bright grin. "Hey, man, this is awesome. So you're gonna dress against Georgia Tech?"

"You betcha. Keep your eye on forty-five, jumpin' up and down on the sidelines."

"Man—this is *some*thin'." They exchanged high-fives. "You know what I'm gonna do? I'm gonna let you win today. That's my present to you."

Rudy shook his head. "It's too cold to play, Garson, and I'm too old—old and beat-up. And wouldn't it be just great if I went and got injured now?"

"Yeah, you're right." Garson leaned against the fence, dribbling the ball. "Well, I got some news for you, too—"

"You went for your interview?"

"Yup. And I'm accepted for next year. Ain't that somethin'?"

"That's somethin' all right!" Rudy grabbed Garson and danced him around the old, cracked asphalt court.

"I'm still gonna be a commercial pilot," Garson said, laughing. "But thanks to you buggin' me for so long, I guess I'll be an educated one. . . ."

The home-game pep rally took place that evening; another bright and golden moment Rudy had been waiting for all his life, it seemed. The team was introduced to the fans and student body, and the seniors were the main focus of attention.

When it was Rudy's turn to be introduced, Coach Devine said, "And this is Rudy Ruettiger, a senior, and a bulldog, though he goes by the nickname Pinball. He gets caromed all over the field, but he always comes back for more. For the past two years he has provided heart and inspiration to our winning cause— and we are pleased and proud that he will dress for tomorrow's game against Georgia Tech."

Rudy stepped forward, waved, and beamed. He was happily stunned that the applause for him was every bit as loud as for Steve Mateus and Roland Steele, two of Notre Dame's most glamorous stars.

In keeping with the Notre Dame tradition, the team spent the night at the Moreau Seminary. Moreau was an ideal place because it was at the far end of the campus, across St. Joseph's Lake, tucked safely away from the noise, the crowds, and, yes, the drinking that was an integral part of football Friday night at South Bend, or at almost any football town in the country for that matter. After dinner, before an early curfew, the team was shown a movie. Rudy was walking on clouds, too excited to follow the plot. For the first time in his life he felt he was where he was supposed to be, that he truly belonged, that he was no longer a stranger staring through a window at the fortunate and privileged few. At last he was *one* of the fortunate and the privileged. Everywhere he looked, there were players—great players, many of them household names not only in South Bend but across the length and breadth of the country—whom he could honestly call his good friends. Mateus and Steele and Joe Montana and Ross Browner and Willie Fry and Steve Nieuhaus, and on and on.

Early the next morning—game day—the team mass was conducted by Father Reilly, and as the team was leaving church to return to Moreau for breakfast, Jamie O'Hare walked up to Rudy.

"Hey, congratulations," he said. "I'm glad you're dressing for Georgia Tech. You really deserve it, you know."

Rudy looked at O'Hare for some sign of the hidden knife, but he seemed sincere. "Thanks, Jamie," he said.

They walked in silence for a moment. Then: "No hard feelings?" said O'Hare.

Rudy took a moment to answer. "Well, maybe a few, to be honest. But you and I can handle that."

"Yeah," said O'Hare, "we can handle it." He cleared his throat. "That's a fine piece Mary did on you. Pretty long for *The Observer,* though. They don't usually run stuff that long."

Rudy smiled up at O'Hare. "You still like her, don't you?"

"Yeah." O'Hare nodded. "A lot. But we've had our problems."

"Well," said Rudy, "I want you to know I'm not one of them. Maybe I'd like to be, but it's not in the cards. We're just friends."

"Oh, I wasn't even thinking anything about that," said O'Hare. But Rudy noticed that he looked relieved.

"Huddle up," said Devine.

It was minutes before game time and the players gathered around their coach. In the still of the locker room, the thumping sound of the band on the field vibrated through the walls, heightening the anticipation of going into battle. Rudy's heart was pounding in his throat, his head. He was sweating from nervousness, from fear, from happiness—from everything. He had to keep reminding himself that the moment was happening in real time, that this wasn't just another dream. He wished Jim Obsetnick could be here with him, sharing this moment. He'd run into him on the way to the stadium. Obsetnick was in civilian clothes, and as they talked he seemed on the verge of tears. Rudy had wanted to say, "You've got so much more talent than me and you should be in uniform for the last home game of your college career," but at the same time he realized that Obsetnick hadn't wanted to dress for a game as badly as he had wanted it. His friend hadn't been willing to give his life for it.

Devine said, "You all know what you have to do. Remember—no one, and I mean *no one,* comes into our house and pushes us around. This is *our* house. We rule here. Gentlemen—this is your game now, and for you seniors it's your last here in this great stadium surrounded by all your loyal fans. Make it count. Make it your very best game, because you'll remember it for the rest of your lives. Don't hold anything back, because there's only this one moment in time, and what you don't give to the game now, this afternoon, you'll never have a chance to give again." He raised his arms and cried out, "Let's get 'em!"

The players started chanting, *"Go! Go! Go!"* as they filed toward the door. Rudy knelt quickly in front of the priest, as did a number of the other players, and was blessed. He then moved over to touch the Gipper plaque, yelled, *"Spirit!"* and then ran down the stairs, a manic grin on his face.

The team gathered in the darkness, waiting for the signal to run out on the field. Rudy bounced up and down; even though he'd stayed awake most of the night, tossing and turning, running this moment through his mind again and again, visualizing it, almost tasting it, he had more energy than he could handle.

Roland Steele hit him hard in the shoulder pads. "You ready, champ?" he said.

Rudy grabbed his friend's hand and pumped it up and down. "Ready? Shit, man, I've been prepping for this all my life."

"Well, my man, you're gonna lead us out on the field."

"Me?" Rudy looked blank, uncomprehending. "I am?"

Steele slapped him on the back. "You're the man, Rudy."

Suddenly the band broke into the Notre Dame fight song—

Cheer, cheer for old Notre Dame,
Wake up the echoes cheering her name,
Send a volley cheer on high,
Shake down the thunder from the sky.
What though the odds be great or small,
Old Notre Dame will win over all,
While her loyal sons are marching onward to victory.

—and the players roared as they burst from the darkness into an explosion of sound and light. Rudy pumped his fist in the air again and again as he ran across the field, his feet barely touching the turf. He looked up into the stands and caught a quick glimpse of his group—Danilo, Frank, Ma, Johnny, D-Bob and Elsa, Fortune, Garson—then quickly looked away and joined the others on the sidelines.

Danilo sat in his seat, looking stunned.

"There's Rudy," said Johnny, pointing. "Number

forty-five. See him, Ma? He looks big in his uniform, doesn't he?''

Betty Ruettiger turned to the woman sitting behind her and said, "That's my son, number forty-five."

"It looks different than on TV, huh, Pop?" said Frank.

"Yeah, it's different all right," said Danilo. "You think he'll get in the game?"

"No," said Frank.

Danilo nodded. "I guess that's askin' too much. This is enough of a miracle."

"Don't count him out," said Johnny.

"It ain't up to him," said Frank sharply.

"Well, I'd never count him out," said Johnny. "He has a way of making things happen."

D-Bob puffed on a long cigar. "That Gipper pulled it off," he said to Elsa. "He really pulled it off. Talk about long odds. But then I shouldn't be surprised. I never knew a guy more hell-bent on getting what he wanted."

Elsa held up *The Observer.* "There's a big article in here on Rudy."

"Who wrote it?"

"Mary McDonough."

"Somehow that figures." D-Bob nodded his head in wonderment.

"Do you know her?"

"A very slight acquaintance," answered D-Bob. "She's a big campus heartthrob."

"Was she your heartthrob, Dennis?"

"Oh no, I was immune to her charms," said D-Bob quickly. "Am I in the article?"

"Believe it or not, yes."
D-Bob grabbed the newspaper.

Against Georgia Tech, the number-one rushing
team in the country, Notre Dame's offense came to
life after weeks of somnolence. They were up 10–0 at
the half, and with three minutes to go in the game Roland Steele intercepted a pass and ran seventy-three
yards for a touchdown: the Irish 17, the Ramblin'
Wrecks 3.

Rudy sat on his helmet saying one mental prayer
after another. He prayed that he would get in the
game, if only for one second of playing time, so that
his name would appear in the record book. Without
his name there, he wasn't sure he would ever again be
completely real to himself. He prayed that his teammates would score a lot of points so that his dream
could come true.

It looked as though his prayers were being answered when the score reached 17–3. Georgia Tech
would need two touchdowns and extra points even to
tie; there was finally a nice cushion, and suddenly a
chance—if only a slim one—that he might get in the
game.

On the sidelines, after Steele's touchdown run, Devine said to Yonto, "All right—three minutes to go.
Let's send in the seniors now."

Yonto slid his eyes toward Devine and yelled over
the din of the crowd, "Ruettiger, too?"

"No."

"Just one play? It would mean a whole lot to him."

Devine shook his head emphatically. "Absolutely
not. We've had scholarship kids here who've never

been in a game. Why should Ruettiger be an exception?"

"Because he *is* an exception," Yonto was tempted to say, but over the course of the season he had learned that Coach Devine did not take kindly to opinions different from his.

The senior scrubs entered the game; Rudy was not one of them. Steele looked along the sidelines toward Rudy, who continued to sit on his helmet, alone and disconsolate. He said to Mateus, "We've got to get Rudy in there. Shit, this is ridiculous. He's earned his shot."

"I'll talk to Coach," said Mateus. "It's my last game. I don't give a damn."

"I'm captain," said Steele. "It's my job."

He walked up to Devine, who paced up and down, his hands clasped behind his back, fell in step beside him, and said, "How about letting Ruettiger in, Coach?"

Devine looked at him sharply. "You, too?"

"He's meant a lot to this team," said Steele.

"First Yonto and now you," said Devine. "Well, the answer is still no. And I must tell you, you're overstepping your bounds."

"I thought I counted for something around here," said Steele, beginning to show his anger.

"I'm the coach of this team," said Devine. "I make the decisions." He moved away from Steele, his arms now hugged tight across his chest as though to protect himself, his mouth tight as a snip of wire. Without another word, Steele stalked back to Mateus, shaking his head.

Suddenly, with one minute forty-five seconds remaining in the game, Georgia Tech fumbled, giving the Irish the ball back.

On the sidelines, Mateus shook his head and moaned. He said to Steele, "Christ, Roland, there goes his chance. The offense is gonna run the game out."

Steele kicked at the dirt hard with the toe of his shoe. "We've got to get him in there somehow, someway."

Mateus pointed at Jamie O'Hare. "Hey, look who's going in. Let's have a quick word with him."

In the stands, Danilo shook his head. "Rudy ain't gonna get in now." His eyes looked red; his jowls shook. "It's a helluva shame, Frankie. The kid got so close and he wanted it so bad."

Frank studied his father. "I think you want it bad, too, Pop."

D-Bob, on his second cigar, was listening to a small battery-operated radio he held up to his ear as he watched the action on the field. The play-by-play broadcaster said, *Here he is now—Jamie O'Hare, the highly touted recruit four years ago takes the field for the final minute and a half of the 1975 season. I think it's safe to say O'Hare's career at Notre Dame has been a bust. . . .*

"He's a prick besides," commented D-Bob, blowing a cloud of smoke toward the sky. "Sorry, Elsa."

She smiled. "The smoke or the cussing?"

"Both."

Garson Faulk leaned forward and said through gritted teeth, "Come on, put him in, put Rudy in. Come on, put him in." Then he stood on his seat and shouted, *"Rudy, Rudy, Rudy. We want Rudy. We want*

Rudy. We want Rudy!'' The chant was quickly picked up by others in the stands. On the sidelines, Mateus and Steele heard the cheers for Rudy, and joined in, yelling, *''Rudy, Rudy, Rudy, Rudy! We want Rudy, we want Rudy, we want Rudy!''*

"Damn," said Devine to Yonto as he prowled up and down the sidelines. "Can't we stop this?"

"Don't know but one way," said Yonto. "Put Ruettiger in there."

Devine frowned, shook his head, and continued to pace.

On the field, O'Hare was in the huddle when a messenger arrived and told the quarterback, "Coach wants you go to on one knee and run out the clock."

The chant of *''Rudy, Rudy, Rudy''* was clearly audible on the field now, ringing out from the stands and the sidelines. The players in the huddle all looked around and at one another.

"Q-Protect on two," said the quarterback.

"Hold up a minute," said O'Hare. "It seems like the only way to get Rudy in the game is to call another play."

The quarterback scowled at him. "You kidding? Go against the coach?"

"Just this one time."

"I got my orders, O'Hare."

Some of the other players joined in, saying that Rudy should get in the game, he'd helped the team all year, he deserved to be in on at least one play.

"Come on, Bob," said O'Hare to the quarterback. "The hell with Devine. If there's any flack from him, lay it on me. He hates my guts anyway. Let's score for Rudy and get back on defense so he can get in. How about it?"

The rest of the huddle roared their agreement. The quarterback glanced nervously toward the sidelines, then said, "Oh, what the hell. My career's over anyway, right? Okay, Jamie, this is yours, man. Wing left, QL-four hook flash on two."

The team broke with a clap.

The quarterback took the snap and pitched the ball to O'Hare for a halfback option pass. O'Hare threw a perfect spiral thirty yards downfield into the waiting hands of his receiver, who eluded two attempted tackles and high-stepped into the end zone for a touchdown.

The crowd went wild. Jamie ran off the field, accepting congratulations. He walked over to Rudy and said, "That was for you, man. Maybe it makes up for some of my shit."

Rudy reached out his hand and he and O'Hare shook. "Thanks," he said. "I won't forget this."

The players increased their chant of *"Rudy, Rudy, Rudy, we want Rudy, we want Rudy, we want Rudy."* Steele stood facing the crowd, waving his arms like a cheerleader, conducting the chant; finally the entire stadium was chanting, *"Rudy, Rudy, Rudy, Rudy . . ."*

"My son," Betty Ruettiger shouted to the woman sitting behind her. "That's my son they're calling for." In her voice confusion, pride, and wonder were all mixed together.

Danilo, on his feet now, holding a Notre Dame pennant aloft, a wide smile stretched across his face, chanted his son's name, as did Johnny and Faulk, who was also jumping up and down on his seat, and

D-Bob—and even Frank. Only Fortune was silent, but a proud and secret smile lit up his features.

On the sidelines Rudy looked around, stunned with amazement, as his name rumbled through the stadium, filling it. He spotted Mary in the press box, leaning forward, screaming his name. He waved and grinned and she waved back.

After chewing out the quarterback and glaring holes through O'Hare, who was carefully avoiding him, Devine approached Coach Yonto. "I guess we put him in," he said.

"I think that's a good idea, Coach," said Yonto. "The game's locked and everybody wants him." He turned to Rudy and yelled, "Get in there, Ruettiger. . . ."

And so, with twenty-seven seconds remaining in the final home game of his career at Notre Dame, Rudy ran out onto the field. The crowd rose to its feet, roaring. A spectator sitting directly in front of Frank turned to him with a puzzled expression on his face. "Hey, who is this Rudy guy anyway? I've never heard of him."

Frank stared at the man. "You haven't?"

"No. And I follow the team pretty closely."

"Well, you're hearing about him now. He's a great little player. Giant heart in a small body." Then Frank added, a tremor of emotion in his voice, "He's also my brother."

On the kickoff to Georgia Tech, Rudy ran downfield and tripped over his own feet before he could get within twenty yards of the kick returner. *"Shit, not now, don't let this happen to me now,"* he muttered as he ran back to line up at defensive end. Across from

him squatted the gigantic Georgia Tech tight end,
ready to spring. He squinted across at Rudy, an un-
pleasant leer on his face. "Get ready, hero. I'm gonna
squash you like a bug."

Rudy smiled back at him. "You and your mother,
pussy. That's the only way you'll get it done."

"Why, you little creep . . ."

As the crowd continued to chant *"Rudy, Rudy,
Rudy, Rudy,"* the Georgia Tech quarterback took the
snap and faded back to pass. Rudy charged hard on
the outside. The tight end swung his clublike forearm
around and knocked Rudy back off his feet. The
quarterback's pass was incomplete.

Eight seconds left on the clock, eight seconds left
in Rudy's season, in his career. The spectators were
on their feet, chanting Rudy's name. One of the loud-
est of all was Frank, who kept repeating like a mantra,
"C'mon, bro, c'mon, bro, c'mon, bro. . . ." And
D-Bob, waving his cigar around wildly, yelled, "Stick
it to 'em, Gipper. Come on, baby!"

The players on the sidelines were also screaming at
Rudy, urging him on. He looked over and gave his
teammates a thumbs-up sign, then took his position
across from the tight end.

"Just wait, you little piece of shit," said the tight
end. "The last one was a love tap."

Rudy winked at him. "You won't lay a hand on me,
lover."

The ball was snapped. The quarterback again backpedaled to get into position to pass. Rudy faked to the
outside, getting the tight end off balance, and then
blew past him on the inside. The quarterback was
clearly in his sights. Only one blocker stood between

them. Rudy did a little stutter step, faked and swiveled
by. With a desperate lunge, he caught the quarterback
around the ankles, bringing him down for a fourteen-
yard loss.

As loud as the roar in the stadium had been before,
it now increased to a deafening pitch; it was as though
the Irish had just won the national championship.

The team rushed out on the field, picked Rudy up,
and carried him toward the sidelines. Atop his teammates' shoulders, Rudy pumped his arms as he
searched the stands. For one brief moment, before the
team entered the tunnel, he and Danilo locked expressions. Both were smiling. Both were in tears.

This is it, Rudy thought. This is the moment. And
it's forever.

In the tunnel he laughed and yelled, "Roland,
who's the king now?"

"You are, baby," said Steele.

"I say Roland, *who's the king*?"

"You are, baby. Lord have mercy, *you* are."

"I say who's the king?" Rudy blasted out like a
gospel preacher, and all the players broke up laughing, their laughter mixing with their cheers.